The Distance

Between Us

a novel by

Jill Breugem

THE DISTANCE BETWEEN US
© Copyright 2018 Jill Breugem

Edited by Darla Wright
Cover Design by Adriana Breugem
Suitcase: RF Clipart by Katya Ulitina
Formatted by Wendi Temporado

Acknowledgements:

Thanks to all my readers for taking the time to read my first book *Read Between the Lines* and joining me for my second book, *The Distance Between Us*, leaving me reviews, recommending my book, and sending me notes of encouragement. #grateful

Thanks to my family for helping me with my *Read Between the Lines* launch party. Your support while chasing my dream meant so much to me! AND oh my - the cupcakes!! #sweetsupport

Thank you to my parents for having so much faith in me; you are my biggest cheerleaders and supporters #loveyou

Thank you to my editor Darla, and my cover designer and sidekick Adriana #youhelpmakeitallcometogether

Always thankful and grateful for my family Jaap, Adriana, Alex and Lucy #myheart

This book is dedicated to my brilliant and beautiful nieces & nephews. You can accomplish anything that you want in life. Follow your dreams xo

Chapter 1

Party

Exiting the elevator, Ally let out a nervous sigh. It was crazy, wanting to see him like this. Her relationship with Gage had just ended. She had sworn off dating for a long time and then she heard that *he* was back in town. Ally always had a soft spot for Oliver.

The elevator doors opened on the top floor to the penthouse suites where her best friend and famous New York Times bestselling author, Sadie Fisher lived. A familiar face was getting off the elevator across the hall at the same time.

"Levi! Fancy meeting you here!" Ally joked.

"You're early," he said.

"So are you." Ally hit back. They were roommates, so it was funny that they had both arrived at the same time, yet didn't come together. They had an easy relationship. Ally had never had a brother but imagined this is what it might be like. She had left Levi's house and popped over to her mom's condo before Sadie's party and would be staying with her mom when the party was over. It was convenient that her mom lived in the building too. Usually she would just stay with Sadie, but thought she just might be a third wheel tonight.

She noticed that Levi looked nervous standing there with a big bouquet of flowers for Sadie.

"I was hoping to have a quick talk before everyone arrived," Levi said, shrugging.

"Shoot, I can go back down to my mom's." Ally knew what it was about. Levi had just learned that Sadie was single and he wanted to be clear about his feelings for her. Ally had always thought Sadie and Levi were meant to be together. After seven years of Levi being her agent and one of her best friends, Ally thought it might actually happen for them.

"No, no, don't worry about it. Come on, let's go in." Levi held his elbow out so that Ally could loop one arm in his. Ally looked at him sideways.

"Really?" she laughed. Ally was juggling boxes of Sadie's favourite gourmet cupcakes and a bunch of huge helium balloons.

"Sorry," he chuckled. "Let me help you," Ally gently leaned in to place a box of cupcakes in his open hand.

Ally hugged her best friend as Sadie opened the door. She was thrilled for Sadie that she was done another book! She was sure it was going to be another bestseller like the ones before, and she couldn't wait to read it!

"Hi!" Sadie exclaimed, giving Levi a hug also. Ally handed her a box of cupcakes and the balloons, and Levi her favourite roses. Levi had been a great friend recently, letting Ally stay at his place while she was going through her ugly split from Gage. An ugly split was an understatement and was letting Gage off far too easy. Gage had gone from what seemed to be sweet and attentive, to controlling and abusive within a matter of months. Ally had fallen hard for him, and unfortunately, ended up on the on the receiving end of a violent rage. She was strong enough to leave and took solace at Levi's while selling her home. She was planning on moving back in with her mom.

Although moving back in with your parents was not on everyone's wish list of things to do, Ally took comfort in being with her mom, and looked forward to moving back home. She also had plans for the money from the sale of her house. She was going to open up her dream store selling essential oil products.

Going to the fridge like she owned the place, Ally grabbed herself a cider and Levi a beer. Placing the drinks on the counter, she went on a hunt looking through the drawers for a bottle opener. Almost wiping her hands on her linen pants she stopped herself and turned on her heel to grab a towel from the cupboard. She was wearing black linen pants and a white wrap top that hugged her curves. A chunky, rose gold, statement necklace finished the look. She chose to embrace her long curly hair as usual and added only a smidge of makeup to her delicate features. Her green eyes sparkled at the thought of Oliver coming through that door at any moment.

Sadie was rattling on to Levi, whom Ally wished she would just hurry up and marry already. The two of them had been playing a love tennis match for seven years, claiming to be just friends. They clearly loved and had the hots for each other. Recently, Sadie had come clean to Ally about her feelings. Levi had more or less done the same. They were both single, and Ally was sure tonight would be the night they took this relationship further. They were meant to be together.

There was a knock at the door and Ally's stomach churned. *Whoa, hope this isn't what I am going to be like all night*, Ally thought. *You can handle this, get yourself together.* Ally was typically the confident one, but her recent relationship had left a mark in more ways than one. She was working on it, and she planned on snapping back. She took a long drink of her cider and as she swallowed and placed the drink back on the counter, she looked right into the eyes of Oliver.

"Hi Ally. It's been a while." *How had he made it over to her so fast?*

Slightly choking and spitting what was left in her mouth all over the handsome specimen in front of her, she gained some control, grinned, and held out her hand. Chuckling to himself knowing what had just happened with the drink, Oliver tugged her hand towards him and engulfed her in a bear hug.

"How are you, Ally? It's great to see you."

"I'm good, Oliver." Blushing, something she rarely did, she added, "It's great to see you too. Sorry, I was choking on my...I think I'm just learning how to drink…"

His warm smile made her forget why she was even standing there or where she was. He still had a slight British accent from his time living in London, England. He was so tall that her head landed in the middle of his chest when they hugged. He had a toned, slender build and dark, short, wavy hair. His eyes were a light blue, but if she looked long enough she could almost see flecks of gold. He had a sexy sprinkling of a five o'clock shadow lining his strong jaw. She thought about biting his full bottom lip. *Where did that come from?* She thought.

"I think I'll put these in the fridge," he said, interrupting her thoughts and motioning to the craft beer he held onto. *Biting his lip?* She thought to herself again, and giggled, hoping he couldn't sense her wicked crush.

"Here, let me," she said, taking them from his hands and turning to the fridge. She didn't realize that he was smiling broadly behind her, completely smitten with her as well.

"So you're back," Ally said, stating the obvious. She took a slow drink of her cider.

"Yes, my stint there is done, for now. I've just moved back."

"I see you two found each other…" Levi teased.

"For now?" Ally questioned, her heart sinking a little. *Silly* she thought, *it's not like you are in love or have a stake in what he does, this is just a crush. And what did Levi mean by that?* Her mind was racing with thoughts.

"Ally was the first person I looked for, after saying congrats to Sadie, of course," Oliver said in a matter of fact tone to no one in particular as Levi smiled and walked over to Piper, another one of their friends and Sadie's publisher. Then turning to Ally, Oliver added, "Yes, I set up our offices there. I hired someone really good to support the team. Don't think I'll need to go back anytime soon, except for twice a year reviews and such."

The first person he looked for? I see you two found each other? Ally was freaking out inside at what Oliver had said to Levi. She noticed he was excited talking about his company. They spoke some more about his business. She was genuinely happy for how successful he had become, starting his business from scratch years ago.

"What are you up to these days Ally? Are you still writing for the paper?" She realized she had to focus on the conversation! *Snap out of it Ally!*

"I am. I also write for some other publications, websites and blogs here and there. I have been putting a little extra into my other interest lately."

"What's that?"

"I make and sell essential oil blends, mostly online and to some friends who feel sorry for me," she joked.

"Oh really? Like perfume?" he asked, genuinely interested.

"Some of it is...here, smell." She leaned forward pulling her hair to the side, exposing her neck. He leaned down instinctively, and smelled the delicate scent of lavender with something sweet and something he couldn't place, some kind of citrus scent.

"You made that? Smells good, Ally. Lavender and…citrus?" Her skin tingled from the closeness.

"Thank you, yes I did. Good nose, Oliver. Lavender with bergamot. There's a bit of vanilla too."

"You smell amazing. Would you make one for me? What would you suggest?" Hopeful, his warm eyes twinkled at her. She didn't stand a chance. *Why her?* She thought. He could have any one of the model types around this room, why short curvy Ally with the red hair and freckles. Then she thought, *why not me?*

"I can make one for you." Smiling at his request, she added, "I would probably use the bergamot like I did for me, but with sandalwood or cedarwood. Something woodsy and fresh."

"Sounds good, you're hired." They talked more about her passion for essential oils and why she loved them so much, as well as her dream to open up her own store.

"I can help you with that. Let me know when you're ready."

"I will. Thanks Oliver."

The night went on and the conversation never stopped. It was like they were the only two people in the room, except for a few interruptions by a few well-meaning friends. She made him coffee when he wouldn't take a beer, laughing over old stories of when they first met.

The evening was winding down and after an early start that morning at a farmers market with her oils, she was fading fast.

"I'm either boring you to bits, or you're wickedly tired," Oliver teased.

"I'm so sorry…no, not bored at all, you're great company. I was up really early today." Ally insisted adding, "I had a great time tonight."

"Me too. I hope we can do it again, not necessarily at Sadie's," he joked. "Can I give you a lift home? We can talk about going out sometime?"

"I'm actually staying at my mom's tonight. She lives in this building. But you can walk me there if you like?"

"I would love too. Let's say goodbye to Levi and Sadie...it looks like everyone else left," Oliver noticed looking around, chuckling.

Sadie and Levi were in a deep conversation of their own sprawled out on the lush couches. They were talking about what cities to go to for the book launch. Levi wanted her to go to London this time. Oliver's ears perked up.

"When are you planning to go, Sadie?"

"Well, Levi is suggesting around January or February."

"Not the best weather at that time of year, but I imagine you don't have a lot of time for sightseeing."

"I've been before, but there are still a few places I'd like to check out."

"We should all go!" Oliver exclaimed looking around the room at them. "Or does that cramp your author stuff?" he quickly retracted.

"Oh goodness no, Oliver. My signings are only a couple of hours long and we can space them over several days or a couple of weeks."

"I love that idea," Levi interjected. Sadie looked over at him, trying to read his expression as Ally sat there with her mouth agape, completely stunned. *Oliver is saying that they should all go to London in February. As a group! The four of them!*

"I think it's a great idea too. It would be a blast having you guys on the tour with me!" Sadie said. "Ally?"

"Sure, sounds good." There was no hesitation from Ally as she looked from her best friend to Oliver.

"Well, I look forward to the planning. Let's get you home Ally." said Oliver.

Chapter 2

Mom

Closing the door quietly so as not to wake her mom, Ally locked up and leaned her back against the door. Oliver had just walked her home. When was the last time a man had walked her home? He was a perfect gentleman. Walking strong and steady beside her with no expectations. Upon reaching the door, Ally no sooner looked up towards Oliver when he took her right hand and kissed the back of it softly. She realized her mouth had fallen open. She closed it into a sweet grin. Oliver winked at her, squeezing her hand before letting it go.

She held her hand up to inspect it closer in the dark, as if there was something that she could see. Then she lifted her hand to her mouth and kissed the spot still humming from the touch of his mouth on her skin. Ally couldn't help but think of what it would feel like to kiss him. He had put her into a spin just by kissing her hand.

"Hi, honey. I just put on some herbal tea, would you like some?" Ally's mom Catriona softly called from the kitchen interrupting her heated thoughts. Ally's face flushed.

Dropping her hand to her side and pushing herself off of the door, Ally couldn't tell if it was Oliver or the ciders she had had earlier were making her feel all woozy. She had a buzz and couldn't wipe the smile off of her face if she tried.

"You're up late, Mom."

"Couldn't sleep. Would you like a tea?" Catriona repeated.

"I'd love one." Ally said and plopped herself into an armchair in the cozy living room. Grabbing a colorful afghan she wrapped it around her legs and curled up on the oversized armchair. Home was wherever her mother was, she thought for a moment, looking around the room at her mother's eclectic and hippie taste. There were natural wood bookshelves full to the brim of books, pictures and tasteful knick-knacks from travels. There were green leafy plants, a Buddha and a diffuser going at all times. It was no wonder Ally had gotten into essential oils and natural living; her mother had been her role model.

"You look like you had a good time, yes?" Catriona handed her daughter a mug of chamomile tea and adjusted the blanket to cover her daughter's toes.

"It was," Ally said and added, "It was a great time," blowing on the hot tea and staring off into space.

"How is Sadie? Did she give more details on the book? When is the launch date? I can't wait to read it. Been waiting for this one." Catriona rattled on, but Ally was off somewhere else. She looked at her daughter, the spitting image of herself. It was like looking in the mirror at her younger self. Same curly red hair and emerald eyes. Catriona had some extra freckles and some lines around her eyes and mouth to show the years she had been blessed with.

"Ally?"

"Hmm, what?"

"The book," her mom said, sitting across from Ally in the matching chair and curling her legs up just like her daughter. "What's gotten into you?" she laughed.

"Sorry, what were you saying?"

"How is Sadie? Did she tell you more about the new book?" Her mother repeated the sentence with a bit more enunciation.

"Oh she's great. But, I didn't talk to her all night. I have no idea about the book," she admitted. Funny, she wasn't even sorry.

"What? How do you go to your best friend's party and not even talk to her about what the party is about?" her mom said, looking at her aghast.

"She was busy herself, Mom, hosting...besides, we talk all the time," Ally justified, suddenly feeling badly. Did she even say congratulations? Did she even talk to anyone else? Oh yes, there was the introductions with Samantha's famous new boyfriend. Samantha was one of Ally's closest friends and an actress who had hit the big time when she was cast in a Hollywood blockbuster.

"Sam showed up with Adam Lane! Can you believe it?" Ally remembered, exclaiming.

"Wow! Adam Lane! Why didn't you call me?" Catriona giggled. Meeting a handsome actor from Hollywood would be exciting for many, but considering she had ran in circles with famous people before, it wasn't that thrilling for her. "Is that why you're all starry eyed? Adam Lane?"

"Oh no, no way, that's Samantha's new man. It was cool meeting him, though."

"Well by the look on your face it appears that you were talking with someone…"

"That obvious, huh?" Ally put her mug down on the side table and held her hand to her mouth again. "Yes. I was talking to someone pretty amazing."

"You still haven't told me who," Catriona said, with a soft chuckle.

"His name is Oliver," Ally said, picking up her tea and holding it at her chin, smelling the aroma of lavender, chamomile, and peppermint.

Smiling, her mother asked, "Is he with the publisher or a friend?"

"He's longtime friend of Levi and Sadie's. I met him several years ago," Ally said, "but shortly after he went to work in London, England."

"Is he back for good now?"

"Oh, I don't know, Mom, all I know is he's here now." She was smitten. She was full on crushing. Catriona knew her daughter well. Sadly her relationships didn't usually last. Ally had been hurt before and didn't have a lot of faith or trust in men. It all started with her own absent father, accompanied by a string of bad relationships in her twenties, including a long term one with a handsome actor named Nate Fox. Ally met Nate through Samantha. They had had a great time, until he broke her heart taking up with an equally famous and gorgeous actress. Ally had had the impression they were more committed than they were. As a result she became afraid of becoming attached and would flee many of her relationships before they got too serious. She had just started to let her guard down for the first time in a long time with her last boyfriend, Gage. He ended up betraying her trust as well. Catriona was surprised Ally was even entertaining the idea of getting close to another man. *He must be something really special* she thought.

"Well, he sure put you in a spell. I do like seeing you like this. You look so happy, Ally."

"We're going for dinner on Wednesday night. But, I know I have to calm down. I'm really not ready for anything yet."

"Well, as much as I think it's always important to take things slow, you and I aren't exactly wired that way, Ally." She started thinking of her own relationship with Ally's father.

"We also might all go to London for a book signing for Sadie, I almost forgot about that!"

"Really? When?"

"I think it's sometime in the new year."

"That will be fun. I have some money set aside you can have for the trip if you need it?"

"That's okay, Mom. I'll have money. I'm selling the house."

"Are you sure?"

"Yes, definitely," Ally answered.

"You know I love having you here. I also know how much you loved that house and having your own space." Pausing she added, "He's gone now and you have a restraining order."

"I know. I just don't feel like its home anymore. I'll find a new place to love."

"Of course. Tell me more about Oliver," said Catriona changing the subject.

Adjusting the afghan on her lap, she cradled her mug of tea in her hands and settled in to tell her mom all the details of the evening.

Chapter 3

First Date

Oliver called Ally within a few days to confirm their dinner plans for Wednesday. They were going to go out for dinner at a trendy restaurant in one of the tall office towers located in the financial district in Toronto. The hotspot was on one of the top floors and provided a beautiful view of the city and harbourfront. Ally had never been there before and was very excited. She knew it was expensive and almost impossible to get a reservation. She wondered what strings Oliver had pulled. He was very successful and likely had some connections.

Oliver arrived at 7:00, parked, and got buzzed in so that he could meet Ally at her door. He had a beautiful bouquet of cut flowers to give her and wanted to meet her mom. The flowers might have been a bit too much for a first date, but he was old fashioned that way and thought every woman deserved some chivalry. Ally was no exception. He had been looking forward to seeing her at Sadie's. He knew she would be there to support her best friend, and was even happier to hear from Levi ahead of the party that she was currently single. He had fallen for her years ago at first sight, but had headed to London and didn't pursue it. He loved her sass and outgoing personality. To say he was attracted to her was an understatement. She was the whole package.

Knocking on the door, he took a deep breath to calm his jitters. Ally opened the door smiling. She was wearing a black knit dress that hugged every curve, with knee-high black boots, and a green scarf that matched her eyes. Her naturally rosy cheeks donned a dusting of freckles that complimented her beautiful red curly hair. She was stunning.

"Hi Oliver, come in." Ally motioned to him, ushering him into the apartment.

Handing her a big bouquet of tulips, the flower that he had heard was her favourite, he softly said, "These are for you."

"Wow! Thank you!" Ally beamed at the flowers, smelling them as she headed to the kitchen where her mother was making a sandwich. "Mom, this is Oliver, Oliver my mom, Catriona."

"Nice to meet you," Oliver said, reaching out his hand to shake hers.

"And you as well. Beautiful flowers, Oliver. I didn't think men did that anymore." Oliver was taken aback by how much the two women looked alike. Ally was the spitting image of her mom, simply a younger version.

Ally reached up on her tippy toes to get a vase that was located on the top of the fridge in a basket.

Oliver smiled and effortlessly reached over to pick up the vase and hand it to Ally. "You have a lovely place. Have you lived in this building long?"

"Thanks Oliver. Moved in here several years ago. Sadie moved in upstairs and told me all about it." Catriona was very impressed by her daughter's date. Incredibly handsome, tall, and charming, she could understand why her daughter was on cloud nine.

Ally's mom leaned in to give her daughter a kiss on the cheek. "Have a great time tonight."

"Thanks, Mom. Ready?" Ally said, holding out her hand to Oliver. He took her hand and gave her a wide, bring-you-to-your-knees smile.

They headed down the elevator in silence. Not in an uncomfortable silence, but in a smirking, winking, flirting way, as Oliver stood on one side facing Ally on the other.

When they arrived at the bottom he said, "You look beautiful, Ally."

"You aren't so bad yourself, Ollie." She wasn't sure if he cared for the nickname, but she went with it, and he didn't complain or make a funny face.

"I'm excited about going to this restaurant," she said climbing into his silver Aston Martin. "Have you been there before? Wow, this is a beautiful car."

"First time for the restaurant and glad you like the car," he said pulling into traffic. "I'm looking forward to it, too," he said, winking again at her. She hadn't smiled this much in a long time. Not even when she thought she was happy with Gage.

"Your mom has an accent - is that Irish?" Oliver asked.

"Yes, it is. My mom came to Canada when I was a couple of years old. She lived here for a short while before I was born, then went back home to have me, but we came back."

"You were born there too?"

"Yes, I was born in Ballymena, Northern Ireland."

"And your dad?"

"Oh Oliver, that's a story for another day…" Her voice trailed off as she stared out the window. He noticed that her voice had changed and there was sadness there. She had also used his full name rather than the endearing nickname she had used earlier.

"Hey, good time at Sadie's the other night, eh?" Oliver quickly changed the subject.

"Yes, it was," Ally looked out the front window, then turned slowly towards Oliver. She was grateful that he didn't ask any more questions or make the moment more awkward than she had made it. "I have to admit, Ollie, that other than talking to you, I don't remember much of it."

"What about meeting *the* Adam Lane?!" he said, adding extra emphasis to the famous actor's name.

"Oh, yes, I do remember that," Ally laughed. "Wasn't the highlight of my night though," she said flirtatiously, smiling at him.

"You used to date an actor, didn't you?"

"Yessss...." Ally emphasized the 'S', rolling her eyes.

"Another story for another time?" Oliver joked.

"I'd say, unless you want to start talking about your ex-girlfriends?"

"Point well taken. Forgive me."

Oliver turned his eyes back to the road, using the stick to gear down for a stop light. *He was beautiful*, Ally thought to herself. Dark lashes naturally curled up from his eyes. His jawline was strong and his mouth smooth and pink. His dark brown hair looked like it had just been cut and a dusting of scruff lined his jaw and around his mouth. His clothes were immaculate. He looked like he had walked out of an Alexander McQueen magazine advertisement. He was wearing a tailored, charcoal grey sports coat with fitted black pants. A checkered black and white shirt peaked out at the collar. He always seemed so put together.

Oliver looked over to catch Ally looking back at him. She felt her skin blush, but instead of looking away, she said "You caught me," and laughed.

"Well, I know where my eyes would be if they didn't need to be on the road right now," he answered, winking at her.

"Is that so?"

"Ally…" He nearly growled her name, and her body responded immediately with a knot in her belly. He reached across her lap, took her hand in his, and kissed the back. It was a similar move he had made the other night outside her apartment, and it gave her the same reaction. She looked down at her hand, now safely back in her lap, still tingling from his touch.

"Tell me about where we're going?" she asked.

"I've never been there before either. I'm looking forward to seeing it with you. Apparently the views of the city are pretty amazing."

"It's the perfect night for it." They chatted on comfortably, parked the car, and made their way inside and up to the top floor of the building. The view was spectacular and the company even more so.

"Tell me about England. Why did you go to London to work?"

"The company had an office there. A position came up in senior leadership and I thought, why not?"

"It's a big move, no?"

"Yes, but…" He paused, considering whether he should explain further.

"But…? Sounds like there's a story there."

"Well, I didn't really have anything to keep me here," he answered. Looking at her straight in the eye, he added, "I met you days before my flight."

"I remember."

"I was pretty bummed to be honest. I was like, damn, I just met this great girl. Timing was terrible," he said, smiling.

"Tell me about it. I bent Sadie's ear for months."

"Oh reeeally...." He was teasing, but very intrigued by this statement. Ally took the opportunity to wink at him and change the subject back to him.

"Did you miss your family?" Ally asked, thinking how she would never be able to leave her mom.

"Of course, but we kept in touch and I came home often. Probably ended up seeing them more than when I lived in Toronto," he answered.

"Yes, I can understand that. You made a point when you come home from London."

"Exactly."

"Your mom and dad live in Toronto?"

"They're in the east end. I grew up in West Hill."

"Brothers or sisters?"

"Yes, I have a sister, Margaret, who lives over in Mimico. She's married to Alex and has twin daughters, Ana and Mellissa."

"I bet you're a fun uncle. How old are they?" Ally pictured Oliver as an uncle and as a dad. She never did this. Ally always lived for the moment and didn't like to think too much in advance. At least not where relationships were concerned.

"I try!" he said, smiling. He was beaming as he told Ally all about them.

"Do you want to have kids one day, Ally?" he asked, as if reading her mind.

"I don't know," she answered truthfully.

"Really?" Oliver asked, concern on his face.

"Just not something I've thought about much," Ally said, and took a large gulp of her drink. This is the conversation that men either decided it was great to have a girl like her who didn't want commitments, or where they decided she had too much baggage to deal with. Usually it wasn't on the first date. But since Oliver and Ally already knew each other, their serious conversations seemed to be several dates earlier than her other dates.

"Fair enough," Oliver said and moved on to another topic. No judgement and no other comments. She would thank him one day for that.

The evening flew by and before she knew it, Oliver was taking her home. He got out of his car in front of the building and came around to the passenger side to open the door before Ally got the chance to.

"Thank you Ollie," she said as she got out stepped up on her tippy toes to kiss his cheek. Oliver didn't move his body out of the way, but closed the car door behind her, moving in closer, one hand gently holding her chin while the other hand rested on the car behind her. Leaning down, he kissed her softly on the mouth. He stepped back to see the reaction on her face. Her eyes were hazy, cheeks flushed, and her mouth hadn't moved since the kiss. He picked up her hand and kissed it, holding it in both of his. Smiling, he nudged her.

"I had a great time tonight," he said.

"Mmhmm," Ally answered. Pushing off of the car that had held her body upright during that kiss, she composed herself. Suddenly, she was wishing she was living at her house and inviting him in.

"I'll call you and we can do this again?" he asked.

"Yes, Ollie. I had a great time too," she said, answering his first comment, and then continued, "And I would love to."

Relief flooded over him, and eased the knot in the pit of his belly. He knew she wasn't quite ready for anything serious. He knew little of what happened in her previous relationship, but Levi had warned him. He wasn't sure if that's what the walls were though. As much as she reciprocated and seemed to be interested, there was something he couldn't quite put his finger on. She just seemed to be at arm's length.

He was so into her and wanted to see how and where this would go. He was prepared to take things slow and he was prepared to work much harder than he ever had before. He knew she was worth it. She was funny, intelligent, and sexy as hell.

Chapter 4

Launch Party

Ally and Sadie entered the romantic bookstore for Sadie's launch party. Candles were lit on antique glass chandeliers and Sadie's favourite roses were placed throughout the room; it looked stunning. Books were stacked on tables and there were waiters handing out glasses of wine. A playlist of songs that likely Sadie listened to while writing the book played over the speakers. These events were set up by the publishing company but they always had Sadie's personal touches.

Sadie told her there would be a big surprise with this book. It wasn't the one she pitched to Levi. Piper had worked with her in the last couple of weeks to switch out the book originally intended for a novel about her and Levi. It was a very bold and romantic move for Sadie to profess her love for him this way. Ally knew Levi would be ecstatic and she couldn't wait for her two friends to finally be honest with each other.

Thinking about them got her thinking of her own feelings for Oliver. Was it simply a crush? Was it just an attraction and nothing more? Where was it going to go? Ally just wasn't a relationship person. She had come to terms with this fact after her relationship with Gage ended terribly mere months ago. She had finally started to trust someone and let her guard down then to have Gage physically abused her to the point of filing a police report. It was a terrible time, and the fact that she was now entertaining a new relationship was crazy. She needed time alone. She needed to grow happy with herself and understand her own issues before going there with anyone. She would be sure to tell Oliver the next time they went out. *Nothing serious. Just a good time. She could do that,* she said to herself.

There he was. He must have come in with Levi, and they were both talking to Piper. Oliver looked so handsome in his fitted suit and skinny royal blue tie. Both Levi and Oliver started to look around the room. Although Ally wanted to wave to Oliver and greet him immediately, she knew she better let her best friend know that Levi was here. They hadn't been speaking recently and she knew that Sadie was looking forward to making things right tonight. She saw that Sadie was over by a table of her books. Her back was to Ally and she was hugging a book to her chest, deep in thought.

Each book was a new baby for Sadie and she understood that this one was just as important as the others, if not more so.

"Sadie…" Ally touched her arm gently.

Sadie looked at her friend with a small smile and tears brimming her eyes.

"I thought you would want to know that Levi is here."

"Yes, thank you," Sadie said, still cradling the book.

Ally watched as Levi and Sadie found each other with their eyes. Levi was headed straight towards her with a look of determination. He clearly wanted to make things right too. Ally moved to the side and made herself scarce as she was handed a glass of red wine from a waiter.

"Hey, you," a familiar voice said to her from behind.

Turning around with a smile she met the eyes of the very sexy and very tall Oliver.

"Hey, you," she answered softly, taking a sip from her wine while looking up at him through her long lashes.

"I called you the other day," he said, as he stepped closer to her.

"Yes, I saw that," she answered. She knew he wasn't used to waiting for women. She had been busy with real estate agents looking at potential locations for her store. She had meant to call him back, but she was making him wait.

Smirking as if reading her mind he leaned down and whispered in her ear, "And, were you going to call me back?" Their bodies were almost touching and his warm breath on her ear and neck just about did her in. She couldn't believe the feeling that came over her. The chemistry between the two of them was intense. Goosebumps seemed to be a regular occurrence for her now whenever she was in his company. She could smell a faint touch of the aftershave she had made him after Sadie's party. Either the wine was hundred proof or she was intoxicated by the mere closeness of him. She couldn't be sure. All she knew was that she was feeling woozy.

"Yes," she answered, and placed a hand on his chest, stepping back to make some space between them.

"Hmmm. I hope so, Ally. I really hope so. You look stunning by the way," he looked down at her and placed his hand over hers that was still resting on his chest. He pulled her hand away from his body and laced her fingers with his. He was admiring the body hugging, nude, lace dress she was wearing. Smiling at her and closing his eyes, he faked falling to his knees, making her giggle. He then nodded to the side and motioned to walk over to where Sadie was about to say a speech. She let him hold her hand. It felt good, but it was also territory that she wasn't used to. He just did everything so effortlessly. He was smooth but not in a way that concerned her. She was scared for other reasons all together.

The bookstore was full, mostly of people she knew. Samantha was there with her new Hollywood boyfriend, Adam Lane. They were currently filming a movie together in Toronto. One photographer and reporter had been allowed to stay for the evening and the photographer was busy taking pictures around the room. Oliver squeezed her hand, bringing her thoughts back to this beautiful man beside her. Why was she freaking out holding his hand? They had only been on the one date so far and they never had the conversation on whether they were going to make it exclusive. She laughed to herself. Settle down Ally, he's only holding your hand, he's not proposing. She looked up at him. Oliver, sensing something was wrong, softly squeezed her hand again, and then let go.

Listening to Sadie saying her speech, professing her love for Levi, was emotional and beautiful. They were meant to be together and everyone knew it. They had driven everyone crazy for years, dancing around their relationship.

Oliver and Ally walked over to them and gave them pats on the back and hugs.

"It's about time!" Oliver announced. "Sadie, this guy has loved you since day one, you're finally putting him out of his misery!"

"Thanks, Oliver," Levi joked, rolling his eyes and pulling Sadie in for another kiss. Soon they were joined by Piper, Samantha and Adam.

"Congratulations on EVERYTHING!" exclaimed Samantha. "So happy for you, my friend," she said, pulling Sadie away from Levi momentarily to give her a big hug.

The two women embraced and swayed back and forth with sheer happiness. Samantha was congratulating Sadie not only on the book, but also on her new relationship.

"You deserve to be happy, Sadie, and Levi is such a gem,"

"I know it, Sam," she agreed. "How are things going with Adam?"

"It's going good...but you know…"

"What?" Sadie asked with earnest.

"Things are great for now, but what about when the filming ends? I live here, he lives in LA, and just not sure it will work. But I'm having fun for now!"

"Focus on the moment, Sam, don't worry about three months from now. Just enjoy right this moment." Sadie looked up and past Samantha to catch Levi watching her sweetly. He smiled when their eyes connected, and Sadie felt the heat rush into her cheeks.

"I need them to change up the music, I want to dance!" Sadie exclaimed. As Sadie walked towards the event planner, Levi caught her arm and turned her towards him.

"Sadie Ann Fisher, where are you going?"

"Who wants to know," she teased.

"This really nice guy."

"Oh really?"

"This really nice, charming guy."

"Mmmm"

"This really nice, charming and good looking guy,"

"And modest?" Sadie teased.

"I'm trying to sell him…"

"Oh, he's sold. Can you tell him I'm going to put on some dancing tunes, because I want to dance with him?"

"Only if you kiss him."

"Kiss him?"

"I've kissed you three times in my life, and I need one more, I can't go another second, Sadie."

"Well, I wouldn't want to torture you," Sadie said wrapping her arms around his neck and leaning her body against his. Levi didn't waste a second to steal a kiss, pull her in tightly, and wrap his strong arms around her waist.

When they pulled away and walked over to the stereo in the back room of the shop, Levi said, "Looks like Oliver and Ally are hitting it off?"

"It does, but…"

"What? What don't I know?

"Ally is complex. I just hope Oliver isn't expecting too much."

"Too much?"

"Like a relationship."

"Really? I think they look smitten with each other."

"Yes, but Gage was the longest relationship she has had since the thing she had with the actor Nate Fox, and that ended horribly. I don't think she's ready for something so soon after that whole ordeal. I know she isn't."

"Fair enough."

"Fair enough, what?" Oliver asked while walking towards the happy couple.

"Oh, nothing…" Levi answered, not wanting to go there at Sadie's party.

"Have you seen Ally?" Sadie asked Oliver.

"She just left, said she'll call you in the morning."

"Everything okay?"

"She said she had a bad headache. I just walked her to a cab."

"That's too bad."

"Hey, Oliver, I saw Jenny the other day at…" Levi began but was interrupted by Oliver right away.

"Not interested, buddy."

Levi looked at Sadie who was averting her eyes on purpose. "Did we get any scotch for this party, Miss Fisher?" thinking to himself how badly he wanted one. His best friend looked like a smitten pup and he had more or less given him the advice to go for it with Ally weeks ago. Now he was learning that that might not be the best idea. *Oliver would have done what he wanted anyway*, Levi reassured himself.

"No, cheapo," Sadie teased. "I'm going to sign some books and then how about we all go back to my place? There's plenty there."

Before getting to the signing table, Sadie texted a quick note to Ally.

"I know what you're doing. Talk to you tomorrow friend xo"

Chapter 5

Jones

As Ally and her mom Catriona entered the foyer of the condo juggling shopping bags, Jones was there within seconds to help.

"Good afternoon, ladies," he said warmly, taking the bags from Catriona while holding the elevator open.

"Thank you, Jones. I've got them from here," Catriona said to him. "It should be the punishment you get for spending so much money." She smiled and looked into the eyes of the dashing doorman.

"No, no, these are heavy. I'll come up with you and take them to your door," Jones insisted. "I would hate for you to hurt your shoulders, Cat." Did he just use a nickname or a short form? Ally asked herself.

"You're too good to me," Catriona smiled and swatted his arm.

Ally looked from her mother to Jones and back again. Were they flirting?

"Don't know what I would do without you…" Catriona said, blushing.

"Don't give it another thought. Whatever you need," Jones said, as he passed the bags over the threshold to Catriona.

Tipping his hat, he was gone and Catriona closed the door. Turning her body, she bumped right into her daughter who was waiting, arms crossed.

"What was THAT all about?" Ally said, her toe tapping with a huge smile on her face.

"What?"

"Mom…" Ally said, rolling her eyes and nodding her head towards the door.

"What?" Catriona asked again, but this time she was trying to hide a smile.

Taking the shopping bags from her mom, Ally headed to the kitchen, laughing. "You have the hots for Jones, you have the hots for Jones!"

"Ally Katherine O'Keefe!" Catriona scolded and laughed at the same time.

"It's okay, Mom. You are a breathing, hot-blooded woman and he's a good looking man!"

"I am not discussing Jones with you, Ally."

"Why not? You asked for every detail about Oliver. Why can't I ask you about Jones?"

"It's different," Catriona said as she pulled vegetables out of paper bags and set them on the granite counter to prepare them for the fridge. "There's nothing to tell you anyway, so I don't know why we're even having this conversation!"

"Mom, when's the last time you went on a date?"

"It doesn't matter. I'm happy."

"Mom, you're young, you should find someone to love."

"I don't need to love anybody,"

"We all want to love somebody!"

"You tell me that, when you can tell me that you love Oliver," Catriona said, regretting the statement almost instantly.

Ally shrugged her shoulders and left the room. She thought about ignoring the comment. She thought about starting an Irish brawl and marching back in there and asking her mother to explain further. Instead she counted to ten and called, "Well, whatever, I saw the way you two were looking at each other."

Her mom couldn't dispute that. She could say what she wanted about Ally's love life, but she couldn't dispute there was some major flirting going on between her and Jones.

"He IS very good looking, I AM human, and yes, I noticed," she confessed.

"I do believe the feeling is mutual," Ally said with confidence. "Worrying about your shoulders. Walking the groceries to the door! Ha!" Ally laughed out loud for effect.

"Ally…" her mother said, as she rolled her eyes and then started to giggle. "Maybe he is a little attentive."

"Well, why don't you ask him to go out sometime?"

"I don't ask men out!" Her mother looked at her as if she had just asked her to staple 'easy' to her forehead. "Besides, I barely know him."

"Then get to know him! Go for a coffee. You don't have to ask him out. Just make him think it was his idea."

"How do I do that?"

"Just casually say something to him, ask him if he likes coffee, and tell him you love coffee."

"You make it sound so easy."

"Trust me, I don't think it will take much. Jones is a smart guy."

"We'll see... What are your plans tonight?"

"My plan was to look at some stores the agent sent over."

"Not very exciting for a Friday night."

"It's exciting to me. Besides, I'm going out with Oliver tomorrow night."

"Where are you going?"

"He's going to make me dinner."

"That sounds lovely. Looks like things are moving right along."

"We've spent some time together recently."

"I'm happy you're happy."

Catriona kissed her daughter on the cheek, then went to the sink to fill the kettle. Motioning to her for a tea, Ally nodded yes.

"I don't believe this. I forgot the tea in the trunk of the car."

"I would say that is the universe helping." Ally winked at her mom and didn't offer to go to the car, so that Catriona would have to see Jones.

"I'll be right back,"

"Take your time, don't rush!"

Catriona went to the elevator shaking her head, giggling to herself and her heart beating a little faster. What had Ally started?

She had dated here and there. None of the dates had stuck and she would generally lose interest. Truth is she liked her own company. She loved her relationship with Ally and her close friends.

She had only ever loved one man in her life and that was Ally's dad Clint, a Major League Baseball Player who she met while waitressing at a bar the players went to after the games. They fell hard and fast and tried to make it work while he travelled all over the US for games. But being young, famous, wealthy, and gorgeous, he found being in a relationship while on the road difficult. When Catriona got pregnant he ended the relationship, breaking her heart into a million pieces. She moved to Ireland briefly, but eventually decided to return to Canada with a toddler. He returned several times around that time, trying to reconcile and see his baby girl.

Catriona and Clint had electric chemistry together. They couldn't keep their hands off of each other. The passion that caused them to love hard also fueled wicked tempers and arguments during their relationship. He still couldn't commit and Catriona didn't like the inconsistency for Ally. She also didn't like how her own heart broke each time he left. It was confusing for Ally each time he would stay and each time he left within months. They came to the agreement that he would leave for good when Ally was eight years old, although he had written letters and called over the years.

Clint set up a trust fund for Ally and sent Catriona monthly payments. Ally learned the circumstances surrounding her parent's relationship when she was old enough to understand. Catriona regretted telling her daughter the truth as she believed it was one of the reasons Ally had such a hard time committing to people herself. She often wondered if Clint and Ally would consider a relationship now that Ally was older.

Catriona knew she had a crush on Jones since moving into the building a few years ago. She had always thought he was married until a recent conversation suggested otherwise. Jones was tall and broad and safe. He had a warm smile and always had something nice to say. He was charming, intelligent, and had a career in the police department for 30 years before retiring to work at the building as doorman/security. He felt it had been a good career and felt it was time to change gears to something quieter than the Toronto Police Force.

Catriona exited the elevator at the parking garage elevator and ran smack into the chest of Jones.

"Oh, I'm so sorry Cat, are you okay?"

"Yes, yes, I'm sorry, I didn't even look. Just heading to my car, I forgot my tea," Catriona blurted in one breath. When did she get so nervous?

"Would you like company? I don't like you young ladies walking alone in the parking garage in the evening."

"Sure," Catriona smiled to herself at the 'young' comment.

A perfect gentleman, Jones held every door and made nice conversation along the way.

"Do you drink tea?" Catriona asked as she pulled the bag out of the trunk.

"I do enjoy a cup of tea," Jones answered, but before Catriona could make her big move, he asked, "Can I take you out for dinner sometime, Cat?"

Thrilled and taken by surprise, Catriona exclaimed a big "Yes!"

"Great! How about Saturday night? I can come for you around six?"

"I'm looking forward to it, Jones."

Entering the apartment she couldn't believe what had just happened. Ally was right.

Ally took one look at her mom and knew, squealed, and gave her a hug.

"Nicely done, Mom! Still got it!"

"Well, I would hope so! I'm still young!" Catriona laughed.

Chapter 6

Making Plans

Ally had seen Sadie's text. The text that Sadie had sent her when she left the book launch party early. Her best friend knew her so well, even though the last thing she wanted to do was admit to Sadie she was right, again. After leaving the party, Ally went straight into her pitch black room, kicked off her heels and climbed right into bed, still wearing the dress that Oliver loved so. Ally's phone lit up her tear stained face while she read Sadie's text. She replied with a simple heart emoji.

Truth is, Oliver was amazing. They went for their first date and it was one of the best times she had. She felt like she could be herself around him. He was interesting and educated and they never ran out of a thing to say. With each time she saw him, she knew she was falling for him, and hard. She was terrified. *It was just too soon. Wasn't it too soon?*

* * *

Several weeks and dates later, she was sitting at his kitchen island with her chin resting on her hands, watching Oliver make her dinner. She didn't know what was sexier, the way he moved around the kitchen with purpose and ease preparing her a gourmet meal, or just the sheer sight of him. It wasn't simply that he was gorgeous either; Ally had dated many great looking men. It was Oliver's confidence and sense of humour that brought her to her knees.

"What is going on in that beautiful redhead of yours, Ally?"

"I'm just enjoying the view," she flirted.

Chopping the lettuce, he looked at her and winked. He had put on a playlist of songs ranging from Mumford and Sons to older REM and U2. The song 'All I Want is You' came on. Oliver set down the knife, dried his hands on a kitchen towel, and walked around the island to Ally.

First he stood in front of her, turning her chair so she was facing him. He then leaned forward, placing his hands on the island behind her. Their lips met in a slow, deep kiss, the kind of kiss that she felt in her belly and thighs. He backed away so he could look her in the eyes. Smiling at her with a mischievous grin, his eyes twinkled as he bit his bottom lip. What was he up to? She wondered.

Holding a hand out, he pulled her into his arms and into a warm hug. Oliver couldn't help but say the first thing that came to mind.

"You really are magnificent."

"You think so?" Ally asked, with her head tilted and a sweet smile on her face. Her hair fell around her shoulders. He lifted one hand from her waist and took one silky tendril between his fingers and thumb. "That is quite the compliment. Puts a lot of pressure on a girl."

"No, no pressure, love," he said and kissed her forehead. "Are you hungry? I've made enough to feed an army and you're no more than a hundred pounds soaking wet!"

"I'm starving, and I love to eat, so bring it on! Everything smells so good."

"That's what I love to hear."

They sat down at his dining table. Like his clothes, his home was impeccable, decorated like a designer had been through it, and maybe they had. He certainly could afford it.

"So tell me more about your dreams of having a store, Ally."

"Well, I already bored you with all of the details about my love affair with oils," Ally joked. "It began during university when I went for an aromatherapy massage."

"Ahhh, massage, I need to go for one." Oliver tilted his head from side to side and scrunched his shoulders in an effort to show he was tense.

"Well, she introduced me to grapefruit essential oil. I just loved the smell of it so much. I enrolled into an aromatherapy course and the rest is history."

He poured her another healthy glass of wine.

"Careful there mister, I'm driving home later." She winked at him.

"You could stay," he said, and smiled.

"Thank you, but I can't," she said, pausing, and changed the subject. "I plan on selling essential oils and instructions on how to use special blends for perfume or stress management, natural home cleaning products, and more."

"Do you have a supplier?"

"Yes, I do. I'll make everything on site. I've taken some business courses to prepare, written a business plan, have banks, lawyers, and accountants involved. I'm ready."

"Sounds like it." He was beaming at her and proud of how prepared she was. "I'm excited for you."

"Thanks, Ollie."

"When is the big opening day?"

"I'm aiming for June. Have lots to do before then."

"Well, I'm here to help, if you need me."

"Thanks, I appreciate that."

When they finished their meal they headed to the couch to watch a movie. They agreed on a comedy, something they would both enjoy.

Before long though it was time to go. Ally pulled him in for goodnight kiss, grabbing at his shirt, and pulling him closer. He then took her hands and gently placed kisses across her knuckles.

"What are you doing over the holidays?"

"My mom and I have spent the last couple with Sadie and her family. Sadie mentioned her parents are going to be in Florida this year, she said something about Levi's cottage."

"That's what I was going to talk to you about. I was speaking with Sadie and Levi the other day. I can drive us up if you and your mom are interested. Lots of rooms up there."

"I think that sounds like a lot of fun," Ally said, and knew her mom would be game to go too.

"I have to go to London this week, but I'll give you a call and we can work out the details. Sound good?"

"Are you just gone for the week?" Ally asked, thinking about how she was going to miss him, yet she just went two weeks pretending to be sick. She knew she had issues. It was a good idea he was going away, it was good to take it slow.

"Yes, I'll be back next Sunday, and then we can head up to the cottage on the Monday or Tuesday if that works for you two?"

"I'll talk to my mom and let you know. Sounds perfect. Good night." She beamed up at him.

"See you soon, love," Oliver said in a slightly British accent as he held the door open and walked out onto the front steps in his sock feet.

Smiling to herself on her drive home at the hunk of a guy she just left, she thought how she couldn't wait to see him again.

Just then her phone beeped. Ally pressed for new message on the console. It played over the speaker.

Miss you already, Oliver had texted. Her heart burst.

***

Ally saw the answering machine was flashing. It always escaped her why her mom kept a landline when the only people that called it were telemarketers and they never left messages. So instinctively, seeing this flashing light, her stomach fluttered and she went to bad places. Is everyone okay? Why didn't they call her cell? Is her mom okay? Is everyone okay in Ireland? The red light flashed at her in despair. Frantically, she rushed to it and pressed play. She wasn't prepared to hear the voice on the other end.

"Hi Catriona, its Nate. I'm looking for Ally. Can you tell her I called? My number is the same."

It took Ally mere seconds to think about what to do next... and that was to hit erase.

She didn't know whether to throw up or throw a vase. He had a lot of nerve! Why the heck was he trying to get in touch with her for? That ship sailed years ago! She knew her mom was listed in the phone directory and he would have no way of knowing Ally's new cell since she changed it after Gage.

She was furious and she was excited at the same time. Her ex-boyfriend, the handsome actor Nate Fox was trying to get in touch with her. Had he never gotten over her? She really liked Oliver, so why did she feel this way in her stomach? Why was he still creating a reaction in her?

She didn't have his number; she had deleted it when they broke up two years ago. He obviously didn't have her number, and her mom wasn't about to give it out. Catriona loved Oliver and was a mama bear when it came to Nate hurting Ally. Ally would give her mom the heads up, not to answer calls from a U.S. number. He would get tired of calling, if he even called again. *He was probably just in town and looking for a hookup. Not happening. Not happening with this girl, no way.*

Chapter 7

Christmas at the Cottage

"Thank you again for the drive, Oliver," Catriona said as the car was put into park outside of Levi and Sadie's cottage. Oliver immediately jumped up to open Catriona's door and then moved swiftly around to open Ally's.

"Such a gentleman you have, Ally," Catriona said to her daughter as she waited by the trunk to get her bags. "Wow!"

Ally knew her mother all too well. After telling her mom about Nate phoning, Catriona was going out of her way to make sure Ally didn't get any ideas.

"He'll do," Ally teased, bouncing up on her toes to kiss him on the cheek after he opened her door. He wrapped his arms around her in a bear hug and kissed the top of her head.

"Thank you, Catriona, but my parents are the ones to thank. Manners were and are one of the most important traits to them."

"Hey!" Sadie and Levi waved from the door. "Glad you guys made it up before the storm,"

Sadie looped her arm with Catriona's, taking her bag and walking her into the cottage. "How was the drive?" she said and kissed her cheek.

"Perfect. I really like him, Sadie. I hope Ally sees what a good guy she has." Pausing she added in a whisper, "You know what she can be like." Catriona whispered.

"I do."

"I'm so happy for you and Levi, Sadie."

"Me too. It's amazing," Sadie gushed. "He's a real gem. I can't believe we danced around it for so long. All this time we could have been together."

"Timing is everything, Sadie. Now is the time."

"So right, Cat. Come, I'll show you to your room."

Meanwhile Levi helped Oliver and Ally with their things and had already cracked open cold drinks by the time Sadie and Catriona returned.

"My parents will be here for dinner time," Sadie said to the group who were in mid-cheer with their drinks.

"Right, which brings us to a lodging issue," Levi said, turning to Oliver. "You have the couch buddy, Ally and her mom have a room, and Sadie's parents have the other."

"Oh, I've slept on worse," Oliver said, taking it in stride.

"I'll take the couch, Oliver. You drove us up here, you deserve a good sleep."

"I'll be just fine, Catriona," Oliver replied, as Ally leaned in to give him a hug. She knew that no one was going to change his mind about the sleeping quarters.

The cottage smelled wonderful. Sadie had just finished some Christmas baking. Cookies and squares decorated platters on the coffee table, beside a stack of books. The fire was burning and quilts and afghans were layered on the back of the oversized couches.

The large windows of the cottage faced the almost frozen lake, and the trees were already covered in a heavy snow. The sun was starting to set across the water. Inside was the perfect place to be with the impending storm.

Soon Sadie's parents arrived. Lucy and Tuck, their golden retrievers, came barreling in ahead of them. They were beautiful dogs and everyone enjoyed their company.

The group enjoyed a great meal. After dinner they gathered around on the couches to let their meals settle before getting out some board games. It took some coaxing to get the guys interested in playing, but before long they were enjoying an intense game of charades. Sadie's parents couldn't help but notice how happy Sadie looked. She was absolutely glowing. They adored Levi, so they were equally thrilled that they had *finally* found their way to each other. Watching them at the cottage, Sadie's mom knew that one day they would marry.

Sadie caught her mom staring at them and gave her a grin. She then leaned over to Levi and gave him a kiss on the cheek. He smiled and pulled her into a side hug.

They had only met Oliver a handful of times, but it was clear to see that he was equally enchanted by the feisty and beautiful redhead who had become another daughter to them over the years. Catriona was like family, too. Sadie's mom knew the famous baseball player, Clint Jackson, was Ally's father, but you wouldn't know it. The genes were strong on her mother's side.

Ally looked around the room. It couldn't have been more perfect. The pups were sleeping in front of the fire, her favourite Elvis Presley Christmas album was playing softly. Oliver and Levi were busy sharing funny stories of when they were much younger. They had the room in stitches. All the people that Ally loved was in one room. Yes, she was falling in love with Oliver...she was falling for him hard.

Christmas Eve rolled into Christmas day. Oliver had given Ally a beautiful necklace with a snowflake diamond pendant. She was in awe of the gift, squealing and wrapping her arms around his neck. Ally gave Oliver front row seats to see one of his favourite bands, The Lumineers. He immediately went and played "Ophelia" on the stereo, grinning and mouthing the chorus "heaven help the fool who falls in love" to her. Her heart was bursting.

Before they knew it, it was December 30th and time to head home. Everyone wanted to get back home for New Years. The four friends wanted to make it to Samantha's New Year's Eve party.

Catriona was missing a special someone and Sadie's parents had plans with friends.

Upon getting home, Jones was waiting to greet Catriona, Ally, and Oliver in the parking garage. He kissed Catriona on the cheek while taking her bags in one hand and her hand in the other.

"Did you have a good time? I missed you, Cat."

"I missed you," she answered blushing, "Yes, we had a great week. How was your daughter's?"

"It was really great. Good to see the kids."

"Anything interesting here while we were gone?"

"Nothing is interesting when you are gone, my dear." Catriona felt her face blush again at his sweet comment.

"You guys go ahead, Oliver and I might slip out to get a couple things," Ally said to her mom and Jones, giving Oliver a sideways glance. Oliver looked at her with a puzzled expression.

"Okay," Catriona responded, barely taking her eyes off of Jones.

"Your house now!" Ally whispered and hopped back into the car.

"What? Why?!" Oliver asked.

"Get your buns in here and take me to your house, Ollie."

"Okaaaaaay," he exaggerated, getting back into the car with a puzzled look on his face.

"It's been too long with too many people always around…" Ally said, her eyes twinkling and her mouth turning into a devilish grin.

"Got it!" Oliver blurted, backed the car out of the space, and flew out of the parking garage.

Chapter 8

Just a Jealous Girl

The next couple of months flew by and before long, the crew had arrived in London for Sadie's book signing after a pretty uneventful flight. They pulled up in front of the five-star hotel The Landmark, and were immediately greeted by doormen. Stepping out in front of their luxurious home for the next few days, Oliver took Ally's hand to lead her through the door.

"Why don't you and Sadie head to the bar, Levi and I will take care of checking us in."

Their luggage was immediately swept away by the concierge to take to their rooms. Ally noticed that no expense was spared for this trip and wondered who was responsible; Levi and Sadie for her book tour, or Oliver and his expensive taste?

Ally by no means had to worry about money, but this place was even out of her typical high budget.

"This place is gorgeous. I hear it has an amazing spa. Why don't we book ourselves in for something tomorrow morning?" Sadie said to Ally, as they walked arm and arm into the hotel bar and restaurant located off of the lobby. The modern, dimly lit space was crowded with sharply dressed business men and women, having a cocktail before going home.

You could see that Sadie's mind was racing as it typically would when she was met with inspiration for a novel. It could happen anywhere at any time; Ally was used to it! Taking her phone out of her pocket, Sadie jotted down a couple of notes and then turned to Ally to see what she thought about the spa.

"I think Oliver had some plans for sightseeing tomorrow morning, but I like your thinking," Ally responded.

The girls sat in a quiet corner of the room and ordered a round of pints for all of them. Ally pulled out her own phone, logged onto the Wi-Fi, and sent her mom a message to let her know they arrived safely.

Two very hot guys entered the restaurant and headed towards their table. *How lucky are we?* Ally thought to herself. Levi slid in beside Sadie and immediately put his arm around her, while Oliver sat down beside Ally and took her hand to give it a squeeze. Ally couldn't believe sometimes just how blessed she was to have met him; he was so special to her.

"I don't believe it!" Oliver exclaimed. He excused himself announcing that he saw someone he knew and went across the room to meet them.

Ally couldn't help but notice it was a she and that she was gorgeous. Ally thought she looked like a model with her long, raven hair, perfect bone structure, full lips, and long lean figure. The mystery woman was almost as tall as Oliver and was leaning in close to speak into his ear; too close for Ally's liking. She was tilting her head back and laughing at everything Oliver said. *He's funny, but not that funny*, Ally thought to herself.

Ally could feel her face heating with jealousy. How could she feel this way, when she still hadn't made a commitment to Oliver?

"Why do you look like you want to kill someone?" Sadie asked as she returned to the table.

"Who, is that?" Ally asked Sadie and Levi, through gritted teeth. With a deer in the headlights look, Levi looked from Sadie to Ally to Oliver.

Shrugging he said, "I have no idea." Whispering under his breath for Sadie to hear he added, "He better freaking end the convo and get back here. She's scaring me!" Sadie chuckled.

Oliver continued to keep the beautiful woman hanging on every word. He must have gotten the feeling that six eyes were intently watching him, because he looked over at the table and didn't skip a beat ending the conversation and walking back to sit down.

"Hey, what's everyone having?" he asked completely oblivious to the fireball beside him.

"An old friend?" Ally couldn't help herself. She wasn't one to dance around things.

"Oh, Hilary, yes, you could say that."

Ally gave Sadie a look like she was going to flip the table any moment. Sadie thought it was best to try to diffuse the situation the only way she knew how.

"Who wants to do a shot with me? We have lots to celebrate!"

"Hilary...Hmmmm...She doesn't really look like a Hilary, she looks more like a ...b," Ally said, as Sadie jumped up and called, "Waiter!"

Oliver, who was starting to get with the program and understand what was going on, turned to Ally and said, "Hilary means nothing to me, if that's what you're thinking, Ally?"

Ally exploded into a fit of fake laughter, as she shrugged her shoulders, saying, "I don't care what you are to each other."

"Okay, well, it looked like it bothered you. I just wanted you to know that…"

"Hi, can we have a round of tequila?" Sadie said desperately, when the waiter approached.

"It doesn't bother me. You must've been telling a good story. She was completely enthralled by every word…"

"Ally," Oliver said looking at her with a grin.

"Funny story was it, I could hear her cackle from here."

"Are you done, love?"

"Do you call her that too?" Ally said, raising her voice, clearly pushing it too far this time.

Standing up, Oliver took Ally by the elbow and led her into a public restroom. She was spitting out vulgarities along the way. Oliver gently nudged her in and locked the door behind him. He calmly asked, "Ally, do you want to talk to me about something?"

"Don't patronize me, Oliver. I saw her all over you, hanging off your every word, laughing at everything you said."

"Ally..."

"Seriously, is she like seven feet tall?"

"Ally," he said again, calmly.

"Well, I won't stand in your way."

"Ally, love, I don't like Hilary that way."

"Well, I understand if you do, she's beautiful."

"Not as beautiful as you, love. Not as beautiful as you. Not as clever with her vulgarities as well," he said, laughing.

"Sorry," Ally shrugged.

"Hilary is an ex-girlfriend. It's been over for a long time. I have never looked back, and neither has she."

"So she is an ex-girlfriend," Ally groaned, wondering how to compete with a beautiful, raven-haired, amazon woman.

"Ally, you have an ex-boyfriend who's a movie star. I'm not worried and you shouldn't be either." If Oliver only knew that the movie star had called and left a few messages over the last couple of months, he might think otherwise.

"Love," Oliver said as he pulled her into his arms, "I'm crazy for you. I want to be with you,"

"Ollie..."

Pushing her up against the door, Oliver took her breath away with a kiss that left no disputing how he felt.

He then opened the door and took her hand to lead her back to the table where their friends had just enjoyed all four shots that had arrived in their absence. Both Sadie and Levi were making lemon smiles with the wedges and looking goofy at each other.

"Everything okay here?" Oliver asked. "Leave you two alone for a few minutes and look what happens," he joked.

"We were entertaining ourselves, didn't know how long you two would be," Levi said, laughing, as Sadie dropped the lemon wedge into her hand and tried to conspicuously fold it into a napkin.

Chapter 9

Signings

The next night was Sadie's book signing at the largest bookstore in London. The group went and did some sightseeing before; Big Ben, London Bridge, Buckingham Palace, and the London Eye. They didn't have a lot of time in London and tried to cram as much as they could into the few days they were there. Unfortunately, it was also typical English winter weather in London, raining the entire time. Ally didn't even try to manage her curls, she just let them be wild and free.

Ally and Oliver joined Sadie and Levi at the book signing for a little while. Crowds of people swarmed them, wanting to get a glimpse of their favourite author. The line for the signing table wrapped up and down the aisles and out the door. After taking some photos for Sadie, Ally and Oliver headed back to the hotel to have a drink and relax before a late dinner.

"I'm so proud of her," Ally gushed, as they got into their London Taxi.

"Sadie has done so well for herself, hasn't she?" Oliver answered, putting his arm around her shoulders. "We're headed to the Savoy," Oliver announced to the driver.

"She really has," Ally added.

"She's proud of you too, you know."

"Me?" Ally asked.

"Ally, of course. You've been a sought after journalist in Toronto for years. You're already so successful with your oils that you're ready to set up a store, because you don't have enough room for production. It's amazing."

Ally sat up a little straighter and smiled, considering his compliments. *Yes, I have done well. I am proud.* Ally's store was becoming a reality and had made a name for herself and her writing as well for the cheeky and honest articles.

"Thanks for saying that, Ollie."

Kissing the top of her head, Oliver pulled her into his side for a hug.

While freshening up, Ally's phone rang with a number that called last week. The number was definitely an American number. Instantly her stomach fell and turned. She decided to place a call to her mom back home, to find out if she had anything to do with it.

"He called, Mom. He called my cell."

"Who called? Someone called you in London?"

"Yes, Nate called. Did you give him my number?"

"No, of course not. Ally, why would I? Why is he calling you?"

"I'm happy now. Why now?" Ally said again, her eyes brimming with tears.

"When did he call? Did you talk to him?"

"No way! It's the same number that was on your machine at home."

"I haven't answered the phone when he calls, I've no idea how he got your number."

"Maybe Samantha, I'll kill her! Never thought she would, but she must've…"

"Well, don't be too hard on her, he was probably persuasive."

"Oh I can guarantee he was. I better run, Oliver's going to be done his shower any minute."

Ally got off the phone with her mom and sat on the edge of the bed. Oliver came out of the shower with a towel around his neck and just his boxers on.

"What's wrong, love? You look like you've seen a ghost."

"No, no, I'm fine," Ally blurted.

"Were you talking with your mom?"

"Yes, just thought I'd check in."

"Ahh, thought I heard you say something about Nate."

Ally's blood went cold. *He must have heard me talking about Nate when the shower stopped.*

"Yes, it's nothing. He's called."

"He has? What does he want?" Ally could sense that Oliver wasn't liking the idea.

"I don't know, I don't want to talk to him."

"But you felt you had to talk to your mom about it; it must mean something, yes?"

"No, it means nothing. I just told her to ignore his calls if he calls there. I've no interest in going down that road again, okay?"

"Okay, love." Oliver softened, sensing this was not the road to go down tonight. Besides, here they were in London, having an amazing time.

"I'm going to have a shower," Ally announced, grateful the conversation was done.

He leaned forward and gave her a kiss on the head. She hopped up off the bed and headed straight into the bath, leaving Oliver standing there watching her go. She seemed distant and frustrated. He hoped this would change because he had big plans for the next few days.

Dinner was quiet, but Oliver made the most of it. Soon he had Ally laughing and forgetting the earlier conversation about Nate. He was falling for Ally hard. He couldn't imagine the egotistical Nate Fox worming back into her life. He would be devastated and he knew Ally would only get hurt.

After dinner they headed to a pub to meet up with Sadie and Levi. It was their last night in London and they had plans to make it a memorable night! There was a live band playing and they were covering the Ed Sheeran song "Perfect". Oliver took Ally's hand and led her through the crowds to a table at the back where Levi and Sadie were already well on their way to an enjoyable night.

"Hi! How did it go today?" Ally jumped immediately asked. She was thrilled for Sadie's success, and personally loved the new book. She had stayed in and had read the book in just days. The romance based on Levi and Sadie's love story had garnered a lot of attention and there were rumours it might turn into a movie. This was super exciting and Levi was handling calls about it constantly. The paparazzi were also starting to capture pictures of the couple when they could, all fascinated by their story. Sadie was a huge success as it was; and a movie deal would put her over the top.

"It went great! You should've seen the women drooling over Levi!"

"No they weren't…" Levi said, laughing.

"Stop! They were too! I think they were more interested in gawking and meeting you than they were to get their books signed!" Sadie said playfully elbowing him in the ribs. Levi continued to laugh, blushing at her comments. He was used to attention from women, but not this kind of attention. He only had eyes for one woman though and he had big plans. He couldn't wait.

"Well, the story… and the story behind the story… has everyone interested!" Ally exclaimed.

Levi affectionately squeezed Sadie's hand and leaned in to kiss her cheek.

"What time do you leave for Paris?" Oliver asked them, trying not to smile and let the cat out of the bag. He had a special surprise for Ally. Levi and Sadie knew and played along.

"We have an early morning flight. Her next signing is tomorrow afternoon."

"No rest...'Sadie rolled her eyes, smiling.

"I didn't plan this one very well. Going to be a busy twenty four hours."

"It's okay, we'll get through it and then we have some time to spend in Paris for a few days before we need to head back. We have the event in New York coming up," Sadie confirmed. "I'm so excited for that one!"

Although she also wished to be going to Paris, that wasn't in their plans. Ally had only budgeted tickets for London. After all, she had a store to open. Before heading home, Oliver was going to take her by his offices and on a tour of the area where he had lived in London.

The group partied on for the rest of the evening and headed back to their rooms late, feeling no pain. They would all be sorry when they had to get up in a few hours for flights and sightseeing.

Nothing more was said about Nate and thankfully he hadn't called again. She needed to check in with Samantha and find out why in the world she thought it was a good idea to give Nate her number. After all Samantha had watched Ally's heart break into a million pieces when he left Toronto with Montreal actress Sasha Fillion. Samantha also knew Ally was dating Oliver, so why would she give Nate her number? Maybe she thought now that Ally was happy it was a good time to get the closure she needed with Nate?

Oliver was one of the most confident men she knew, but she saw a completely different person when Nate's name was mentioned, and she could hardly blame him. Nate was gorgeous, although Ally would argue that Oliver had him beat there. Nate was a successful actor and was regularly splashed in entertainment news, thankfully Oliver was not in the gossip magazines. Everyone loved Nate Fox. Everyone but Ally. Still, she couldn't figure out why she felt a twinge in her belly when she thought about him. Maybe she did need the closure?

Chapter 10

Paris

Once at the airport Oliver told Ally he had a big surprise for her.

"What? What is it, Ollie?"

"Here, you need this when you show your passport," he said, as he handed her a boarding pass. She looked quickly to the airport at the top of the pass.

"Charles de Gaulle!" Ally said, letting out a squeal. "We're going to Charles de Gaulle? We're going to Paris?"

"Oui, oui," Oliver said with his best French accent, and winked.

"Oliver!"

The security motioned her through the metal detector as her belongings went through the screening. Using a wand up and down her body the guard then motioned her through to meet Oliver waiting on the other side.

"Your mom knows by the way."

"She does?"

"And Sadie."

"Seriously?" she said, stopping them both in their tracks and pulling at his arm to make her point.

"Oui, oui," he said again.

"Oh," Ally said to herself, thinking that Sadie never gave anything away. She certainly didn't look like she was harboring a secret this big! Paris! Sadie and Levi were already headed there, she had to admit she had been feeling very envious. Although ecstatic, a part of her was freaking out. As amazing as Oliver was, and as much as she knew she felt like she was falling in love with him, this felt like a huge deal, a really huge thing to do. His generosity was overwhelming at times. It reminded her of her dad and how his absence was felt except for the money he sent. It also reminded her of Nate, and how it was all extravagance and excitement until he left her with a broken heart.

Noticing the excitement leaving her face, Oliver swooped in and said, "Hey, we're going to have fun. Don't let that beautiful head of yours start thinking too much."

Relaxing a little, Ally gave him a small smile and then jabbed him in the ribs.

"A little much though, no?"

"What? I've the means, I know you've never been to Paris, and you told me you wanted to go," he said, stopping them before they reached the gate. He turned her towards him, engulfing her in a hug and kissing the top of her head. "Why can't a guy just do something romantic for a girl he's crazy about?"

Ally hugged him back tightly, looked up at him with her emerald coloured eyes, and whispered, "Yes, thank you." Stepping up on her tiptoes she launched herself up to kiss him. A smile spread across both of their faces as he said, "Let's go!"

Taking her hand he led her to the gate where they were accepted right away into first class. Before long they had arrived in the city of lights and took advantage of it being early in the day.

"I can't believe we're here," Ally said, as they walked hand in hand up the Champs-Elysees. She held onto Oliver's arm tightly, letting him guide her along the busy street. Even in winter, the streets were full with people bustling about. He was her tour guide, having been to Paris too many times to count over the years for his company. They had just left the Louvre, the world's largest museum, where Ally got to see the infamous Mona Lisa painting by Leonardo da Vinci. She was surprised by how small the painting was in person, but impressed nonetheless. They were headed towards the Arc de Triomphe. Along the way they passed many shops that she would ordinarily want to run into but she was so overwhelmed by being there, she didn't know where to start.

Oliver was exceptional at reading her mind and tugged her hand, pulling her into a shop called "Lunettes Solaire Boutique".

"You need sunglasses?" Ally asked, thinking it was the last shop she would personally be checking out on this luxury avenue, one of the most famous streets in the world. Louis Vuitton, Tiffany, Chanel, and he picks sunglasses?

"Yes, I forgot mine back in Toronto, and didn't notice in London since it rained the whole time."

She let go of his hand and went off to wander about, looking at the ladies' glasses. Glass cases, marble floors, crystal chandeliers, and white walls; Ally looked around the room and admired how elegant it was for a sunglass store. Picking up a pair of Cartier glasses on a royal blue velvet sash, she immediately put them back after noticing the 5,000 euros price tag. She felt slightly nauseous for touching them. Her face heated; she knew this store was more than a little out of her budget and comfort zone.

But there was her rich boyfriend trying on pair after pair, not even looking at the price tags. The blonde sales woman was leaning forward on her elbows, cleavage falling from her silk blouse. To say she was flirting was an understatement, but Oliver didn't even notice. Coming up behind him, Ally put her arms around his waist, tucking her head up under his raised arm. He dropped the arm to hug her while holding the glasses up to his eyes with the other. He then tilted his head down and kissed the top of her head. Ally sent stink eye to the French woman, who took the hint, stood up and straightened her skirt.

"Quelle paire voudriez-vous?" She said, asking which pair of glasses he wanted.

"Je vais prendre ceci, merci." Oliver answered handing her a pair of Tom Ford aviators.

He spoke fluent French? He was always surprising and impressing her. Was there anything this guy couldn't do? After running his hands through his dark, thick hair, he patted his flat, six pack stomach and turned to Ally.

"How about lunch?"

"Ca sonne bien," Ally answered trying her best to pull from her high school French. He winked at her and taking her hand, led her down the street to an elegant bistro. The aroma of freshly baked bread and savory soups took over her senses. Oliver ordered them red wine and sparkling water to have with their meals.

"Do you have any idea the effect you have on women?" Ally asked, while leaning back in her chair and crossing her legs.

Oliver's face flushed slightly as his sexy eyes bore into Ally's. His mouth turned into a warm smile as he said, "There's only one woman I hope I'm having an effect on."

"You didn't answer my question, Ollie."

"She was trying to sell me a pair of sunglasses. That's her job."

"Yes. Sunglasses. Except she wasn't saying anything. She was, however, showing you her boobs." Ally couldn't help herself. She didn't want to create another jealous episode like she had in London with Hilary, so she laughed while shimmying her upper body at him.

Oliver responded with a laugh and then a whistle, wink, and smile. Ally blew him a kiss.

"You know, Ally, I could ask the same of you."

"Ask me what?"

"The effect you have on men." Nate Fox came to mind, but he pushed the green monster down.

"Whatever…" Ally countered.

"You know exactly what I'm talking about." Leaning forward on his forearms, Oliver confidently looked back at Ally, his light eyes sparkling at her through his dark lashes. The waiter interrupted the passionate tension by filling their goblets with water. Oliver sat back, resting his hands on his thighs. Ally didn't move, instead she gave him a sexy smile with a twinkle in her eye and took a long drink.

***

After some more sightseeing they decided to head to their hotel. They would freshen up for a romantic dinner and stroll to the Eiffel Tower.

Over the next couple of days they shared many tender moments and captured sweet memories in photographs. Ally saved one in particular as her screensaver. It was a black and white photo of the two of them taken in front of the Eiffel Tower. It looked like it was taken right out of a picture frame at the department store. It was perfect.

But, why did Ally still have a nagging feeling? Why was she giving off those vibes to Oliver?

She felt nauseous at the thought of talking or running into Nate. He had called her cell again. Why was he still calling? She was confused by the nagging feeling in her belly when she thought of Nate. She wanted to be with Oliver, didn't she?

Chapter 11

The Break Up

They had been home from Paris and London for a few weeks. It was a magical trip and one that Ally and Oliver wouldn't forget anytime soon. Yet Oliver could feel Ally slipping away. Since getting home she had become quiet and was immersing herself in the upcoming launch of her store. Oliver understood there was a lot of work getting a business started, but he couldn't help but feel it was more than that, especially after an awkward discussion about Nate one evening at his place.

"Has he called again?"

"Has who called again?"

"Nate."

"Yes."

"Have you talked to him?"

"Would it matter?" Ally was feeling bold and tired.

"I think it does, yes."

"You don't trust me?"

"It's not a matter of that."

"Well, what is it?"

"Try seeing this from my point of view."

"And?"

"Would you be okay if a beautiful Hollywood movie-star ex-girlfriend called me?"

"How do I know one isn't?"

"Ally..."

"Don't push this, Oliver. It's getting tiring."

"Tiring for you?! I used to be a pretty confident guy, but I find myself wondering these days. It drives me crazy."

"Oliver! I'm a grown woman. If I want to talk to Nate I will. But I haven't. Okay?"

The conversation continued to spiral downhill. Ally shut down, Oliver spent time backtracking and apologizing. He had pushed her too far and she was making him pay for it. But he was the one who should be upset, shouldn't he? Even Ally knew this.

In the coming weeks when he tried to make plans she was busy with her new store or not feeling up to it.

Ally also flew off the handle when he tried to offer financing for the store. He had no idea that money was going to be such a sore subject. He couldn't say anything right. He didn't know how she felt about being offered money from others stemmed from the exorbitant amounts her father would send her mother to make up for not being in their lives. Ally refused to take money from anyone, including her father, so when Oliver offered, her back went up immediately.

Oliver had pushed her last button talking about her dad and offering her money for the store. He didn't know the half of it, how could he defend him like that? And why did he think she needed his help?

Ally stormed out of Oliver's home and straight for her car.

"Ally, wait!" Oliver followed. His words fell on deaf ears as she continued to throw her bag on the passenger seat and start the vehicle.

"What is this all about, Ally. Come on, open the door." His hands were on the door handle, jiggling it, but she had locked the door. Instead of looking at him, Ally put her head on her arms on the steering wheel.

"Come on, Ally. I don't know what I did wrong," Oliver pleaded to the closed window, knowing she could hear him through it. It was very cold and Oliver had run outside with no shoes or coat on.

With tear stained cheeks, Ally sat up and unlocked the door. With his socked feet crushing the snow below him, Oliver went around to the passenger side and climbed in.

"You're going to get frostbite," Ally said, as she threw the car blanket on his lap.

"I don't care about frostbite. I do care about you leaving, leaving like this. What did I say, what did I do?"

"Nothing."

"Well, it can't be nothing. You don't leave without saying goodbye if it was nothing."

"I'm messed up Ollie." He took comfort that she used his nickname and that she referred to him affectionately.

"We all are," Oliver said softly while taking her hand in his. *Did she still love Nate? Was she about to say that she still loved Nate?* He was freaking out inside. *Please don't do this Ally.*

She allowed the contact for a few moments, then pulled her hand out of his grasp and placed it back on the wheel.

"Ally, I've never tried this hard to stay in a relationship before, and we've only just begun."

"Then don't," Ally whispered. She didn't know what she was doing. She was frustrated and confused about everything all at the same time.

"But I want to. I feel like we have something special. I'm crazy about you," Oliver stated matter-of-factly, turning his body to face her.

"I told you, I'm messed up," Ally said, with a single tear sliding down her cheek.

"Why don't you tell me why? Why not talk to me and we can see if we can work through it together?"

"Oliver, you can have any girl you want. Why do you want to go through this? Women throw themselves at you everywhere you go. You don't need me."

"I don't need you Ally. I want you. I'm crazy about you."

"I'm freaking out."

"Maybe we're moving things too fast, why don't we slow them down a bit."

"Too fast? Oliver you took me to Paris! We've only been dating for a few months!"

"We're more than just a number of days or months, Ally."

"You know what I mean…"

"I told you, Paris was not a big deal. I have the means, I thought it would be fun. It was, wasn't it?"

"You know it was…"

"You had a great time, right?"

"Yes."

"Then what's wrong?"

"I don't know. You also shouldn't push your money so much. I can take care of my store on my own."

Oliver put his hands up as if to say that he plead guilty.

"Ally, I love you. I probably have since we stood in Sadie's kitchen talking about anything but her new book at her book party. Heck, you knew I was crazy about you years ago before I moved to London! I'm not ready to throw in the towel and I don't think you are either."

Trying to take her hand, Oliver continued, "Would I like things to go a lot smoother, yes, one hundred percent. But if it doesn't, that's okay. As long as we can talk and work it out and learn about each other, that's fine. If you need me to slow the train down more than this, I can do that, too, and I won't say another word about the money."

"Our relationship has been spent flying here and there...parties, London, Paris, more parties... It's not real life. It's not reality. Everyday people can't do this." *Except people like Nate*.

"Why do we need to be everyday people? I know you don't want to be known for your famous father or the money he has and that you were given. You've tried really hard to disassociate yourself."

"I am not discussing my father with you." She was angry. She was angry and shaking. Oliver had hit a nerve.

"Ally, you know what I meant, I didn't mean that in a bad way," Oliver said, trying to explain.

"It doesn't matter what way you meant it." Ally's words cut into him.

"Can we turn off your car, go inside, and talk about this?"

"No." Ally wanted to be firm.

"Okay, but we should be able to talk, Ally."

"No," Ally said again.

"Why not? This is crazy!" Oliver was losing his patience. He let out a big sigh and turned towards her in a huff. This only aggravated Ally more.

"I think we need to break up," Ally blurted.

"What?"

"You heard me, I need you to get out of the car now." Her voice was strange, it didn't even sound like Ally.

"Ally…I told you, I love you."

"Please go. Please get out."

"Ally, I am not getting out. We are going to talk about this, this is ridiculous."

"I'm not being ridiculous, get out of my car."

"Ally, I didn't say you were being ridiculous, I said this is," he pleaded, raising his arms and waving about to make his point.

"Same difference, Oliver. I'm the one asking you to get out of my car. I will say it again, get out of my car. I'm going home. I don't want to talk about every little thing and I don't want to work it out, okay? Get out." *What am I doing?* Ally said to herself, even she didn't even know.

Oliver sat there, stunned. How could he respond to that? How could he respond and protect any dignity he had left? Without saying a word, he reached for the door handle and exited the car. He closed the door as softly as possible and stood on their in the slushy snow. In his socks. Hands shoved in pockets, shivering, watching the woman he loved drive away, knowing in his heart that she didn't want this any more than he did.

Her eyes blurred with tears, Ally drove back to her mom's condo. *Did I just let my Irish temper get the best of me? This is what I want, isn't it? Did I just leave the best thing that ever happen to me standing there? What have I done?*

Chapter 12

The Restaurant

Since the breakup, Oliver had remained quite low key. Meanwhile, Ally had already started dating. Ally dealt with things the only way she knew how. She pushed her feelings down and moved on. Sadie didn't like that she had already started seeing other guys so soon, but when she tried to talk to Ally, she would change the subject. As feisty as Ally came across and how she usually spoke her mind, when it came to her own problems she was eerily silent. She knew Ally was just trying to keep her mind off of Oliver. She also knew that Ally was trying to keep her mind off of Nate. Ally had filled her best friend in on the calls from actor Nate Fox.

Sadie knew Ally was confused about how she was feeling about Nate calling. Sure Nate was gorgeous and Ally had really cared for him once.

Once. At the end of the day she really liked Oliver and was too stubborn to admit she may have been hasty in her decision. Breaking up with Oliver wasn't going to change the way she felt about him. As far as Nate went, they both knew he would be gone again. He wasn't serious material.

Ally was going to have to figure it all out. Now that Sadie and Levi were a couple, they all hung out together. Ally had made herself scarce the last few weeks, but she wouldn't be able to do that forever. There was going to be some party or some occasion that she would need to have interaction with Levi's best friend.

Oliver asked Sadie and Levi to join him for dinner, hoping to get some insight from Sadie about Ally. It wasn't fair putting his friends in the middle like this, but it was Oliver's only hope as Ally wasn't returning his calls. Knowing her history with Gage, he didn't want to push it more than he already did. So far the conversation had stayed pretty light.

"Any more signings lined up, Sadie?"

"Just New York City left. That's going to be my biggest one to date," Sadie confirmed.

"They're expecting a big turnout for that one," Levi added. "I'm really excited, I love New York." Levi smiled to himself. He loved going to New

York with Sadie. This would be the first time as a couple, and he couldn't wait; he had some surprises up his sleeves.

Oliver, who had been interested, was now clearly distracted.

"What's up, bud?" Levi asked him.

"I don't believe this." Oliver said, seething.

"What?" Levi and Sadie said in unison, following Oliver's eyes across the busy restaurant to a table where Ally sat with her date, Michael.

"Ouch," Levi said, looking back at Oliver as Sadie winced.

"Who is that, Sadie?" Oliver spit out. If he continued to carve the piece of meat on his plate any harder, and it was sure to break the plate.

"Ahhhhhhhhhh…" Sadie stalled. It wasn't a secret but it also wasn't her business. She felt terrible for him. She knew how he felt about Ally and knew Ally felt the same way.

"Sadie," Oliver pleaded, wanting to know who the man was sitting across from the woman he loved. Levi looked at her softly, knowing this couldn't be easy for her. Resting a hand on her thigh, he squeezed; he would support her either way.

"His name is Michael," Sadie answered, not taking her eyes off of her salad.

She shifted in her seat, uncomfortable. What were the chances they would end up at the same place? Of all the restaurants in Toronto. There was no lack of amazing places to go to. This city had become known as a foodie haven for its range of cuisine and popular hotspots.

"When did this start?" he asked.

"It's their second date. They went out last week," she replied, taking a large gulp of her wine. She knew he was thinking of the timing of their breakup. "They only met a week ago," she added, knowing it was still going to hurt, but at least he didn't have to wonder.

Oliver placed his utensils down on either side of his plate. He sat up straight, finished his wine in one swift drink, and then placed his hands on the top of his thighs. He didn't take his eyes off of Ally. He stood up, no expression on his face, his fists clenched.

"What, was Nate busy?" Oliver spit out, through gritted teeth.

"Whoa, what are you doing, Oliver?" Levi asked. He sensed his friend was looking for a confrontation. Sadie looked from Ally to Oliver and back to Ally. Worried there was going to be a scene, she grabbed her phone and texted Ally a quick message.

"Ally - we are here. Oliver sees you." Sadie watched as Ally picked up her phone and read the message. She placed her phone back down and looked around the restaurant. She found them. She found their table and she looked right at Oliver.

Sadie looked frantically back and forth between them, wondering what Oliver was going to do. Ally didn't look away. Her date didn't seem to notice and chatted on. Knowing her best friend so well, she couldn't help but see that Ally looked like she was going to cry. Oliver and Ally were having a staring match, and Sadie had no idea on who would look away first. It was so intense.

"Nothing. I have to go." Oliver opened his wallet and dropped two hundred dollars on the table. "This should cover dinner."

"No, Oliver, we've got this," Sadie exclaimed. But Oliver had already turned on his heel and walked out of the restaurant. Ally watched him, but she didn't make a move.

"Well that was awkward." Levi tried to joke, smiling softly at Sadie.

"That was terrible. I had no idea that she was going for dinner here."

"It's okay Sadie. Everyone is going to be fine and they are going to have to get used to seeing each other with other people. It's a little soon in my opinion, but Oliver is a big boy."

"I just don't understand what she's doing. I know she loves Oliver. She's acting ridiculous and I have no idea why."

"You and I both know she hasn't had a whole lot of men in her life that she could trust or count on. And you've said it before, she just doesn't let men get close to her."

"She has you and she trusts you. Oliver has given her zero reason to feel that he would ever let her down. I don't know why she panicked. I don't know what she's doing," Sadie stressed. "Should you go after him?" she said, pointing towards the door.

"No, no, he'll be fine," Levi assured her, squeezing her hand.

"He just looked so angry."

"I need him to cool off before I talk to him."

Sadie looked across the room at Ally who was visibly upset. It looked like she was telling her date that she had to go. She was also standing up to wave the waiter over. Her date looked stunned. Poor fool. *Who knows what she told him,* Sadie thought to herself.

Do you want to talk? Sadie texted Ally.

Not tonight. Call you tomorrow xo, Ally replied.

"They'll be okay, Sadie." Levi could see the worry in Sadie's eyes. His beautiful girlfriend always wanted everyone to be happy, everyone to get along. Sadie gave him a sad shrug and continued on with her salad.

***

Stunned, Ally couldn't take her eyes off of Oliver. Instantly she felt the regret for everything. The break up, ignoring his calls, the date she was on. The pain in Oliver's eyes was visible from across the busy restaurant. He was standing with his fists clenched at his sides. Was he going to come over here and fight the completely unsuspecting and innocent Michael?

Ally met Michael while looking for rental properties for her business. Michael happened to be looking at a property at the same time. He wanted to open a microbrewery and happened upon the space with a real estate agent at the same time as

Ally. Although the agents were mortified, Michael and Ally had a good laugh and took the tour around the space together. By the end of it he had asked her out, and because Ally wanted to forget Oliver, she said yes.

She didn't want to forget Oliver. Actually, it was almost impossible to not think about him every second of the day. She had really blown it. There was no way he would take her back now, and she had too much pride to find out. Yes, he had called, but she didn't have the nerve to be confronted. What would she say?

"Michael, I have to go," Ally blurted out, interrupting Michael mid-sentence.

"What?" Michael said with his mouth hanging open, full of salad. His fork was dangling midair, a perplexed look on his face. *This was for the best anyway,* she thought. Looking at him right now she wanted to scream.

"Sorry, you finish, I'll grab the waitress and pay my half on the way out. I have an emergency."

"Well, when will I see you again?" Michael asked, mouth still full of partially chewed greens. *How about never*, Ally thought to herself, but instead answered, "Why don't I give you a call?"

Oliver had left. Instead of walking over, he threw what looked like money down on the table and stormed out. She didn't know what she was going to do, but she caught up with the waitress, paid and then raced out of the restaurant, hoping to find Oliver outside. He was nowhere to be seen. Ally dialed his number, terrified of what he would say, but knowing she had no alternative. She needed to see him and needed to make this right. She called several times, but Oliver was making a point. Her calls went straight to voicemail.

Chapter 13

Moving On

"You're home early." Catriona said to Ally, who barged into the apartment and went straight for her room. "Ally, is everything okay?" she asked as she followed her down the hallway.

Ally went into her room, dropped her bag and jacket on the chair and flopped on her bed.

"What happened to your dinner with Oliver? Are you two okay?"

"I wasn't with Oliver, Mom."

"Oh, girl's night? How is Sadie?"

"I wasn't with Sadie, Mom."

"Oh."

"Oliver and I broke up a couple weeks ago."

"You did? You never said," Catriona said and sat down on the edge of her bed.

"Well, I haven't really wanted to talk about it."

"Do you want to talk about it now?" Catriona gently said, laying her hand on her daughter's back.

"I messed things up, Mom."

"Did you tell Oliver that?"

"No," Ally said between sobs. "Tonight I went out for dinner with some guy, and Oliver saw us. He looked so upset."

"Did you break up with Oliver?"

"Yes, but then I regretted it."

"Who did you go on the date with?"

"Michael, I met him last week. I just wanted to forget Oliver. But then I saw him tonight, and it crushed me."

"Why don't you call Oliver and explain?"

"I tried. He's not answering. It's done."

"Oh, Ally."

"The look on his face today... It's too late. I should have apologized weeks ago. And I should never have gone out with Michael."

Catriona didn't say anything. She just listened as Ally cried through the stories that led up to the break up. She wanted to take all the pain away. She wanted to tell her daughter that it wasn't entirely her fault that she had these issues with men. Catriona hadn't exactly been a good role model. But for now, she just listened and stroked her daughter's back, playing with her thick, red hair.

"We all do things in life at some point that we regret, unfortunately."

"He was the one. I know this now. He was the one, Mom."

Catriona couldn't help the tears that escaped her eyes as she tried to comfort her only daughter. Perfect and imperfect. Complex and predictable. Confident and insecure. She knew that Ally's relationship with Oliver was something special. Ally had said as much to Catriona at Christmas. Catriona had been worried about how soon she had entered into the relationship with Oliver after her previous relationship. And she had worried some more when she heard Nate was calling her again. But seeing Ally and Oliver together, she knew that they were right for each other and it had put her mind at ease. If only Ally knew at the time and not learned the hard way, as she was now.

"Oh, sweetheart. Let me run you a bath and get you a tea."

"Thanks, Mom," Ally said through a sob.

***

It took Levi a moment to determine the sound of his vibrating phone at 8:00 on a Saturday morning. Rolling over towards his nightstand, Levi reached his arm over to grab his phone. Squinting at the screen, he didn't recognize the number.

"Hello."

"Hey Levi, its Oliver."

"Where are you calling from, what number is this?"

"I'm using my parent's line, stayed here last night. Lost my phone there a couple weeks ago before we had dinner at the restaurant."

"That sucks! So, what's up?" Levi said, rubbing his eyes with the back of his fist.

"Just catching a flight at Pearson. Wanted to let you know before I left."

"Let me know what?"

"I'm going back to London."

Levi sat up in bed and adjusted the pillow behind his back. Looking down at Sadie sleeping he was reminded how lucky he was. He had loved this girl for seven years before they finally got together six months ago. Seven agonizing years of watching her in other relationships and bad timing.

"What? Why? We just got back."

"I'm moving back."

"What?"

"Yes, I've been busy getting everything set up, or I would have called sooner."

"When are you going? Today?"

"Yes, movers will pack up the rest of my things. I'm having it sent to my parent's house."

"You sold your loft?"

"I'm going to sublet it for now. Have an agent looking after it."

"Why, man?"

"Do you even have to ask me that?"

"Oliver - it's a rough patch," Levi said running his fingers softly along Sadie's exposed arm. Her hand had moved and was laying on his thigh. He would like to put a ring on that finger someday soon. He didn't need to wait a standard amount of time of dating. They had been best friends for seven years before dating.

"It was...that is until I saw for my own eyes that she has already moved on."

"It's only been a few weeks," Levi said, trying to sway Oliver, but his choice of words fell on deaf ears.

"Precisely, it's only been a few weeks!"

"You're going to leave the country because of that, though? Dude..."

"Careful Levi, she is not a THAT."

"You know what I mean," Levi said, running his hands through his wild bedhead.

"Yes, I do. The company has been having issues with leadership for some time and there was an opportunity to go back and do some restructuring. It was perfect timing.

He was moving back to London, and Levi didn't really need to ask anything more. It was done.

"I'll talk to you soon then?"

"You bet. I'll be back sometime in the summer to see my parents. I'll call you up. We should get together."

"You bet," Levi repeated. Then they said goodbye.

Levi rolled onto his side to face Sadie, who was waking up.

"Good morning, beautiful."

"Good morning," Sadie answered sleepily. "What's going on? Who was on the phone?"

"Well, he's headed back to London." Levi said, shaking his head.

"Who?"

"Oliver."

"What? Oliver? Really?"

"Yep."

"What?"

"He's moving back to London."

"Back to London?"

"Yes, he leaves today."

"Oh that really sucks." Sadie rolled onto her back and stretched her arms up above her head.

"I guess a broken heart will do that."

"Do what? Move to London?"

"Irrational and spontaneous things."

"You have experience with this kind of thing?"

"Yes. I recall a time I made some bad calls when my heart was broken," he said kissing her hair.

"Levi," she said in a soft tone. "You and I both know there was a sequence of events that neither of us were in control of."

"It still happened," he said, pouting.

"Well, has he moved there, or just headed for a visit to his company?" Sadie asked.

"Moved."

"Moved?" Sadie asked again and sat up in bed. Her stomach started to twist for her best friend. She knew she would be heartbroken, whether she admitted it or not.

"Moved. He has sublet his home for one year and he told me appointed a Vice President to oversee his North American offices. He has moved." Oliver had been working out all the details in the past couple of weeks. When he decided something that was it. He had told Levi that he had made the decision upon leaving the restaurant.

"Well that sucks."

"Yes, but gives him time to clear his head and move on."

"He doesn't need to move on," Sadie corrected.

"What?" *Women are impossible* Levi thought to himself and rolled onto his back. *How on earth was anyone supposed to decipher that?*

"She's dating other people, Sadie," Levi pointed out.

"Yes, but that means nothing."

"Again. What?"

Sadie picked up her phone and texted Ally to meet her for coffee in an hour. She started to get out of bed when Levi wrapped an arm around her waist, pulling her back in close to his body.

"Stay..."

"I'm going to go meet Ally and let her know about Oliver." She had to admit she was tempted, though.

"Can't you just text her?" He selfishly didn't want them to get out of bed.

"No! I can't just text her!" She knew he was kidding, but she raised her voice nonetheless.

"Why not meet her for lunch then. I need you," Levi said, whining, and kissed his way up her bare arm.

"No. You'll survive!" She turned and kissed the tip of his nose and headed to the shower.

Looking back over her shoulder she gave him a 'what are you waiting for' look. He jumped up, not skipping a beat.

Chapter 14

Regrets

The usually comforting smell of coffee and baked goods failed to calm her nerves today. Sadie checked her phone, looked outside, and looked around the busy coffee shop. She sipped on her tea while she waited to give the news to her best friend. She struggled with how she was going to tell her, knowing Ally had been through so much over the last year.

Should she just blurt it out? Should they visit for a little while first and then ease into it? There was no good way. She was not looking forward to this conversation, but if there was anyone who should deliver the news to Ally, it was her best friend Sadie. Meeting at journalism school at Ryerson University over ten years ago, Ally and Sadie had shared everything, from their heartbreaks to their dreams and aspirations. They had become each other's chosen family, they spent every holiday and most of their days either together or with some form of contact. They were soul sisters.

"I got your coffee already," Sadie texted Ally.

Although Ally had broken up with Oliver, Sadie knew deep down it wasn't what she really wanted. It wasn't what Ally wanted at all. Ally was madly in love with Oliver and it was freaking her out. Ally had commitment and trust issues. Sadie tried to talk some sense into her after Ally admitted to breaking up with him, but once Ally had made her decision, there was no changing her mind. She was independent and stubborn, and had made this decision rashly, in Sadie's opinion.

Ally's major trust issues with men likely stemmed from not having a strong relationship with her own father, or any man for that matter. Her mother never got into another serious relationship and all of their family was back in Northern Ireland. Add to that a string of bad relationships, leading to years of not committing to anyone. Until Gage came along. He said and did all the right things for her to let her guard down, long enough for the relationship to turn abusive. Who could blame Ally for being scared and cautious to get serious with someone again? Her relationship with Oliver was going at the same lightning fast speed as it did with Gage; Ally had been feeling less and less in control, something she swore she would never let happen again.

Ally entered the coffee shop and gave her friend a warm smile to her friend as she walked towards her table. She threw her camel coloured coat over the back of the chair and pulled her cream scarf off, resting it on her lap. Ally didn't have a stitch of makeup on and she looked stunning. Sadie admired the perfection of Ally's skin with just a dusting of freckles on her creamy complexion, her long lashes, and amazing green eyes.

"Hey, how's it going," Ally said leaning across the table for a hug.

"Fine, here," Sadie said as she pushed the coffee across the table, tucking her golden hair behind her ear, leaning back in the chair, and crossing her arms.

"Thank you, you have no idea how much I need this," Ally said, grinning, though she couldn't help but feel Sadie had something on her mind.

"Well…," Sadie began and was quickly interrupted.

"I haven't been sleeping, Sadie. I keep thinking about Oliver seeing me with Michael. It makes my stomach hurt so badly. I don't even like Michael, Sadie, you know that."

"You might need something stronger than coffee for what I'm about to tell you, then," Sadie said gently.

"What?" Ally's face went white. Regret covered her like a blanket.

"It's Oliver,"

"Is he okay?" All of a sudden bad scenarios started weaving through Ally's imagination. "What happened, Sadie?"

"Yes, he's fine…well physically fine."

"I saw him leave. I've been meaning to talk you about that. Like I said, I just feel sick. I need to talk to him. I need to explain. He's not taking my calls."

"Yes, well…" Sadie tried to continue.

"He looked like he was going to come over and hit Michael! He just stared at us. I left immediately after, went home, and cried with my mom for hours."

"Ally, I am so sorry, hun." Sadie put her hand across the table, squeezing Ally's. Ally's eyes were filled with tears.

"Well…it's just been so...so...intense lately. I just needed to breathe. Michael was a stupid distraction."

"So, you do love Oliver?"

"I do, Sadie, I know I do. And he told me he loved me...and then I left him."

"When was that?"

"At his place the night we broke up. I was so mad - not really at him - but about my dad, and I was confused and I just didn't want to talk about it anymore. He pushed me too far."

"Did you tell him that?"

"Yes, but I wouldn't accept his apology, I wouldn't let him explain."

"Oh Ally…"

"Yes, and it's all been moving so fast." Sadie nodded.

"He wanted to put money towards my store. Like I can't afford it or something."

"Oh," Sadie said, knowing her best friend enough to know that would drive her crazy.

"Still, I hope it's not too late."

"Oh Ally…"Sadie reached across the table again, grabbing both her hands.

"What?"

"It's too late, my friend."

"Why? You know Michael is nothing serious."

"I know that."

"What? Has he married someone already? What is it?"

"He moved back to London," Sadie blurted out.

Ally's face went pale again. Her eyebrows furrowed in the centre and her full mouth was in a thin line.

"What?" she asked.

"He moved back to London, today."

"Just like that?"

"I'm sorry."

"Why would he do that?"

"I think he's pretty heartbroken, Ally."

"Fine, run away Oliver, better I know now that he would do something like this."

"He didn't break up with you, Ally, remember that." It was a harsh thing for Sadie to say.

"Just like my dad, going gets tough…"

"He also had an opportunity to do some work at his company."

"It's only been a couple weeks. He just decided to go?"

"I know, but I guess he figured you moved on already, with Michael. He had the opportunity to work there and he took it," Sadie said, gently.

With her lip trembling and eyes filled with tears, Ally bravely put on her coat and scarf.

"Ally…"

"I'm going to head back home. I have to speak to my lawyer about the spot I'm looking to purchase." She was shutting down.

"Ally, talk to me," Sadie pleaded.

"Nothing more to say. He's gone. That's done." Ally took a long drink of her coffee and walked across the room to throw the cup in the garbage. Sadie watched her, then followed her to the door.

"You wanted to call him, so why don't you? Levi will have a number to reach him?"

"No, that's okay. He's already left, he's gone."

"Ally, on second thought, I don't believe it's ever too late," Sadie offered. "This will all be a

distant memory soon, you two will work it out."
Looping her arm in her best friend's arm, they
walked home to their building in silence as small
sobs escaped Ally's throat.

***

Since hearing the news about Oliver, Ally threw
herself into making her store a reality. She found the
perfect location, signed a lease, and began to
receive large shipments of packaging. She worked
with a local graphic designer to come up with a logo
to represent her company and was excited about the
brand she was building. The containers were a mix
of dark royal blue glass and stainless steel. Her
labelling was in a vibrant lime green.

Lime was one of her favourite smells and
recently, she had begun mixing the essential oil
with others to come up with scents that were
invigorating yet calming to the anxiety that she had
been dealing with lately. One mixture that was
made into a roller-ball included lime oil with
soothing lavender. Another mixed lime with the
honey scent and tranquil properties of copaiba to
make a signature scent.

It was all starting to come together. Her dream
was manifesting before her eyes. Sadie had been
over several times through the week encouraging
her to focus on what she had been building over

several years. It was, after all, a thrilling and exciting time for Ally. One she had been wishing and planning for, for years.

Some girls dreamed of Mr. Right and marriage and babies. Ally dreamed of owning her own store. After her and Gage split up, she sold her house and moved back home with her mom where she felt more secure. With the money sitting there in the bank it was clear to Ally what she needed to do. She needed to turn her dream into a reality. Her mom's kitchen was running out of space to mix her products and she didn't have the space to be storing supplies. Ally named her company "Blend" years before when she began selling from her website. Her store sign was arriving and she couldn't wait to meet the sign company tomorrow when they were going to hang it.

Ally grabbed a stack of mail her mom had left for her. Inside one envelope were tickets to attend Samantha's premiere for the movie that she was starring in with Adam Lane. They had been to premieres with Samantha before and they were always a great time, but none were of this Hollywood caliber. It was another thing for Ally to look forward to and take her mind off of Oliver, she thought, as a tear streamed down her face.

Chapter 15

Return

Ally could barely contain herself as she turned the key in the lock. Her store. Her very own store. Ally had settled on a location on Bloor Street. She was tucked in nicely between a lingerie store and a quaint bookshop that Sadie often used for intimate book launch signings. It was the perfect spot and she was so excited for her upcoming opening.

She longed to be sharing her big day with Oliver. How she wished she could make that right and tell him how sorry she was. She had cried herself to sleep every night since learning the news of him moving to London.

Looking around her new store she felt a bittersweet tug of emotions. She was so thrilled and so sad at the same time. She wanted Oliver with her right now, his strong, tall frame engulfing her in a comforting hug, his warm eyes calming her with just a glance, his strong jaw and full lips twisting in a smile to melt her. She pictured his hand taking hers and leading her through the store, stopping in the back room, and lifting her with his strong arms onto the table, kissing her senseless.

But he wasn't there. He was across the ocean and he may never forgive her. Their love had developed fast and strong in a short amount of time. Oliver had been honest about his feelings from the start although it took Ally longer to face hers.

The tears streamed down her face as sobs escaped her throat. She set her bag down on the big block wood counter, tossed her keys beside and pulled off her coat. Wiping her face with her hands, she ran her fingers under her eyes and pushed up the sleeves of her grey sweatshirt.

It was time to get to work. Pity party was over. There were boxes of supplies and decor in the back room and there was always one thing that made her feel better, and that was making her products. First she needed to set up the processing area. Opening boxes of essential oils, carrier oils, and soap bases, Ally filled her shelves and cupboards, the pain leaving her for a moment.

Admiring the stainless appliances she had picked up for the store, she smiled at the thought that they were better than she had in her home. Some recipes required heating and cooling so it was important to have them in the shop, and she wanted only the best for this venture. She pulled on an apron and threw her long, red, curly mane into a high, messy bun. Her red eyes shone the brightest green as she caught her reflection in a mirror from the bathroom.

Opening the fractionated coconut oil she began to look through her essential oils to make some rollerball blends. She chose to make an uplifting and happy blend and reached for the grapefruit, bergamot and orange to start. Ally poured the drops into the coconut oil and stirred with a stainless spoon. As the fragrance wafted up to her nostrils, her eyes closed and her full pink lips turned into a smile. She was going to name this blend "The Sadie" after her best friend who always had a smile. Naming the products after people she knew was going to be a lot of fun. Her friends and family had no idea and wouldn't know until the grand opening. "The Oliver" scent was going to be difficult to make. Not because it was hard to create, but because it would surely stir many emotions as it was the blend she had made for him when they started dating. He had worn it ever since.

Placing a dozen rollerball containers into a holder, Ally poured the sweet citrus scent into the small glass jars. The balls were inserted and lids tightened. They would be ready for labelling. Making a note to remind her on a scrap piece of paper, she set the oils aside.

She jumped in her skin and her thoughts were interrupted from a knock at the front of the store. Ally was confused as to who it could be, since her mom was out with Jones, and Sadie was in New York with Levi. Samantha was off doing interviews in L.A. ahead of the premiere in Sundance and she hadn't told anyone else the big news yet. Pulling the apron over her head she wiped her hands clean and placed it on the counter as she made her way to the front.

Ally only made it halfway to the door staring at the person on the other side of the window. She was frozen, unable to move another step, her eyes locked with the man she hadn't seen in two years. Like standing in concrete, she was paralyzed. The look on her face went from shock to utter disgust.

He stared back with a much softer look than Ally. He was still as handsome as she remembered. She saw him in the entertainment news often, so she knew what he looked like. But something about seeing him standing there in person, mere feet away... it knocked the wind out of her.

What was he doing here? How did he know where to find her? Samantha? Again? Why would she betray her like this? No amount of grapefruit oil was going to uplift any emotion in Ally right now. She was mad. She was flaring. She was ginger, Irish temper mad as hell.

Ally turned and stomped her way back to the rear of the store, out of view of him. Trying to collect her breath and stop her bloody hands from trembling she picked up her phone and texted Samantha as she couldn't physically talk to her right now.

Samantha - why is Nate Fox standing outside my store right now? It was bad enough you passed along my phone number, but now you sent him to my store?

It didn't take Samantha long to respond. *I didn't tell him where your store is, or what your number is. Sorry hun, but it wasn't me.*

Really? Ally texted.

Really, haven't seen him in ages. Besides, I wouldn't do that to you.

I'm sorry that I assumed. I better go and see what he wants.

Now what was she going to do? He knew she was there. She couldn't hide in the back room forever. Peeking around the door frame she saw Nate still standing outside the door, flowers in hand.

Ugh.

Ugh, ugh, ugh.

Taking a deep breath Ally stood tall, straightened up her sweatshirt, took her hair out of the high bun, and walked to the front door.

She didn't look at him this time. She just walked to the heavy glass and wood frame door and unlocked the bolts. A chime rang as she opened the door wide, stepping to the side and waving her hand to offer him to come in. He hesitated only briefly, smiling as he walked in and over to a counter.

"These are for you," he commented, holding the bouquet of yellow daisies towards her with one strong hand holding them at the base.

"What are you doing here?" Ally asked, bluntly.

Ally looked up and into his eyes briefly, but she didn't want to get caught there too long.

"Take these, and I'll explain." Nate said.

"I don't want your flowers, Nate."

"Come on, it's an exciting time for you. Just take them."

"Thank you." She rolled her eyes, reached out, took the flowers, and then walked past him to the back room. Finding a vase in her decorating supplies, she added water and put the daisies in half-heartedly. She then walked back out to where Nate stood and put the flowers on the counter beside him. She dropped the vase just enough to make the water splash.

Nate shifted his feet, hands clasped in front of him. He was wearing loose jeans and a black shirt under his rugged black leather jacket. His hair was jet black and cut short. He had brown eyes lined with thick black lashes. Yes, he was still gorgeous.

"Been a long time," Nate said in a husky tone to Ally. She stood there staring him down. Her flaming red hair hung at her shoulders, anchoring her petite frame to the floor. Her feet were shoulder width apart and her hands were now on the curve of her hips.

"You could say that." She wasn't going to let him off the hook. She shifted her body weight to one side.

"I owe you a big apology."

"Oh really?" Ally said sarcastically, her tongue in her cheek.

Ignoring her tone, he continued. "Yes. I would love to spend some time with you and talk."

Wow, did he have a lot of nerve, she thought to herself. *Seriously, what could he possibly say and after all this time.*

"Little late, don't you think?"

"Yes, I do. But I still would love to talk to you and explain."

Ally couldn't believe her ears. What could he want to explain? Sasha drugged him? Sasha kidnapped him? Sasha coerced him? What?

"Well, as you can see I'm a little busy getting ready for my store. The grand opening is only a couple of weeks away. I have lots to do," Ally said, waving her arms around the store for effect.

"I could help?" he offered.

Ally defiantly said, "No, thanks."

"I know it was a shock, me showing up like this. I'm going to be here for a while. If you want to talk, you can call me at this number. I'll drop everything." Nate took a pen and paper out of his inside pocket, the sound of crinkling paper and pen clicking echoing in the empty space. Besides that,

Ally could hear her ever growing headache pounding in her ears. He wrote down his number and pushed it towards the flowers.

"I have things to do, so…" Ally said, not looking at him.

"I understand." He paused, then said, "I hope you call." He turned to look at her once more and then was gone. She locked the door behind him and headed to the back room, shaking. Between Oliver going to London, getting the store ready, and now Nate walking back into her life like this, she was feeling very overwhelmed.

Nate Fox. She had fallen in love with him during a week in France at Cannes. She had gone to the film festival there to hang out with Samantha but ended up spending it with Nate instead. They had locked eyes across the room at a party the first night. She had only seen him in magazines and on the silver screen before then. There she was holding her glass of champagne, listening to Samantha and another actress talk shop, when she looked up and right into the eyes of the famous, and famously handsome, Nate Fox. He told her that he had noticed this gorgeous redhead in her tiny, silver mini-dress, but it was her bored expression at a prestigious Hollywood event that had piqued his interest. They spent the next week holed up in each other's arms.

The new relationship continued back in Toronto for several months while Nate finished up filming a movie there. They spent their time at the Ritz Carlton and her house. They managed to keep it secret and stayed out of the tabloids. He lavished her with attention and gifts and she brought him down to earth with her spunky personality and straight shooting attitude. Mutual friends joined them for dinners and parties, and they appeared to be the happiest couple around. Her mom and friends were thrilled for her.

Then one day he said it was time to go and kissed her goodbye. Just like that. It would only be a couple days before he was splashed all over the magazines with Sasha on his arm. What had she been thinking? Did she really think a big star like him would fall in love with her?

Pulling a bottle of wine out of her bag that she had bought for the opening, she grabbed a plastic red cup and poured herself a healthy sized glass. She then climbed up on the wooden counter, sitting cross-legged, and began to think…and drink.

Chapter 16

Sweet Dreams

Ally opened her eyes and felt a sharp pain behind her eyes from looking directly up at fluorescent lights on the ceiling of her shop. Sting. Ache. Ouch.

"Damn." Ally said aloud. Licking her lips she tried to find moisture. Her mouth was dry. So dry. Like someone had held a hair dryer to her mouth as she slept. Where the heck WAS she? She went to stretch her arms, and realized she was still holding a cup with about a sip of wine left. Setting the cup out of the way, she sat up. Whoa...bad idea. Pounding headache. Nausea also hit her. Her body was telling her what a stupid decision she had made, drinking wine, sleeping on the hard wooden surface of her work table in the back of her store, under fluorescent lights.

It all came back to her. Nate. Opening the bottle of wine. Looking through Pinterest. More wine. Drunk texting Oliver. *Oh, Oliver*.

What time was it? When did she fall asleep? Ally patted all around her until she found her phone. It was 10:00. Shoot. She had slept all afternoon and evening! No wonder she felt like throwing up, she hadn't eaten all day. No breakfast, no lunch, and she had slept through dinner.

There were missed calls from her mom. No reply from Oliver. *No reply from Oliver. He wasn't ever going to forgive her*. He didn't return her calls the days following the incident at the restaurant and now he wasn't even answering her texts. Even the drunk ones.

Nate. Nate. It took her a year to get over Nate, and now he had waltzed into her life again just like that. Just like that she felt so confused.

Ally put her phone down, ran to the washroom, and began to dry heave. Her eyes watered as she sat on the lid of the toilet seat, resting her elbows on the bowl of the sink. She was thanking herself for cleaning the bathroom first. Being sick is bad enough, let alone being sick in a dirty bathroom. Running the water ice cold, she cupped her hand to sip and splash her face. Drinking during the day, alone and on an empty stomach, was the stupidest decision she had ever made. Well, maybe not the stupidest, but it was up there. She felt pathetic. Oliver must think she was pathetic too, that's why he wasn't returning her texts or calls.

She needed to get home, and more importantly, she needed to get some food in her belly. She threw water on her face, grabbed a bottle of water, and shut down the store. Locking up, she knew she couldn't drive home. Although she wasn't likely over the alcohol limit after sleeping all afternoon and evening, between her headache and nausea, she was in no shape to drive. She hailed a cab.

The drive took twenty minutes, and thankfully Jones was nowhere to be seen. Ally decided to send her mom a text and go stay at Sadie's apartment while Sadie and Levi were in New York. This way she didn't need to face her mom and talk about Nate. She didn't want to go there right now.

Ally had a key to Sadie's apartment and an open invitation. She sent her a text to give her a heads up. Sadie replied and told her to make herself at home. And she did; she went straight to the kitchen where she buttered a slice of bread with peanut butter and had a large glass of orange juice. When she was done, she headed to the master bath to have a long soak. Putting on the intercom stereo, Ally found an acoustic mix to lull her.

Everlong, Plush and a number of other songs followed. Ally's mind was wandering. It was wandering in places she didn't want to go. She hated this side of herself. She was typically an outgoing, happy and confident person. Not the person who fell asleep on a wooden counter after drinking wine on an empty stomach.

Poking her foot out of the bubbles, Ally used her toes to turn on the hot water again. She had been in the bath long enough for the water to cool. When she got out of the tub she searched Sadie's drawers for a pair of track pants and a t-shirt. She piled her damp hair into a messy bun and used some moisturizer, thankful in this moment for a best friend like Sadie who wouldn't judge and only offer support. Ally loved her so much for that.

Ally grabbed another water, took two acetaminophen, and went to the spare room. The room followed a similar colour palette like the rest of the condo, in greys, whites, and turquoise. This room also had some sunny yellow mixed in. Beautiful handmade quilts and pillows from Sadie's mom covered the queen size bed. A plush grey carpet laid at the side of the bed, matching the grey fabric headboard. A shiny lacquered yellow dresser was the focal point of the room. Knowing that sheer white curtains weren't going to keep out the morning light, Ally pulled the blind down.

Emotionally spent, Ally turned off the stereo and climbed under the covers. She focused on thinking about her store to keep her thoughts from turning to the men in her life; the many that she didn't want to see again, and one that she missed terribly.

***

Good morning, Ally, her mother wrote, *I hope I can see you before I head to work.* The text was sent at 7:30. It was now almost 11:00.

Sorry, Mom. Slept in.

Will I see you tonight?

Yes

Love you, talk to you later

Love you, too.

Still no texts from Oliver. And nothing more from Nate, thank goodness.

Gathering her dirty clothes and locking up, Ally headed down to her mom's condo. She would have another shower before writing a column for a popular blogger. She was a writer like Sadie. They had both worked for a small paper before Sadie went to novels and Ally began her freelance work writing for as many as a dozen publications a week. She was in demand, yet had time to create her own schedule so that she could focus on her business. That worked for now, but once the store was open she knew she would need to cut back.

Grabbing her MacBook, Ally fired it up and made herself a smoothie. She checked her email for the details around the column. It was a spot about worst date ever. Ally knew immediately what she was going to write about. She put a comical spin on the atrocious dinner date with Michael and the love of her life across the room.

Initially she thought it would be painful to write. Instead she found herself giggling at the idiocy of it all. What was she thinking? Many times throughout Ally's life she had sat here like this, shaking her head at the decisions she made.

Catriona came home to see Ally closing her laptop, a huge grin on her face and fist pumping.

"Am I ever happy to see you happy!" Catriona said to her daughter.

"That was one of the easiest and funniest columns I've ever written," Ally squealed and jumped up, kissing her mom on the cheek.

"Can I read? What's it about?"

"I'll show it to you later. Let me make some dinner."

"Okay, what did you have in mind?"

"I'm going to make soft tacos, sound good?"

"Yummy, sounds good to me," Catriona said with a smile. She was always inspired by the way her daughter could bounce back. She worried that she wasn't fully dealing with things though.

"I'll set the table, Ally."

Chapter 17

Proposal

Levi had wanted to do this for as far back as he could remember. Literally since they first met. They had gone out for a drink for a business meeting to talk about Levi representing her as a literary agent. They had talked effortlessly, laughed for hours and he had been smitten with her. To say she was beautiful was an understatement. Sadie was the woman of his dreams, his best friend and soulmate. It sounded so cliché, but he had never felt this way with anyone before. He felt his coat pocket to make sure the little blue box was still safely there.

Sadie and Levi loved New York City and had been coming for book signings for years. Levi never missed a chance to join Sadie when she came to New York. They had shared some great memories over the years there. It seemed fitting to take her to the one spot they visited every time they came to New York and the backdrop of so many romantic movies that Sadie cherished. They loved this city, and loved the views.

His heart pounded as they travelled up to the 102nd floor, the highest observation deck of the Empire State building. He had a few different things up his sleeve tonight that he had carefully planned and coordinated. He wanted the night to be perfect.

Sadie looked beautiful in a coral sweater that hugged her curves, a navy and cream coloured scarf, and navy cropped pants with nude, suede, high-heeled ankle boots. She was almost as tall as Levi with her shoes. She was wearing her long golden hair down in loose waves. As always, she took his breath away.

"I'm so excited to come back here again, Levi," Sadie whispered in his ear, squeezing his hand. Her breathe on his earlobe was enough to make him wish the elevator had been empty. But, it was full of tourists just like them.

Could she sense something was going to happen? Levi wondered if she was she trying to calm him with the hand squeeze and the whisper in his ear. *Could she hear his heart beating outside of his chest? Were his nerves going to get the better of him?* His hand felt sweatier than normal and his body was fidgeting more than usual.

Keep it together, Levi, he told himself. *You got this. You know she feels the same way.*

The elevator opened and Levi could feel his chest go tighter. Were his knees shaking too? Knowing that he was being ridiculous and not trying to be ridiculous were two different things. Levi wasn't able to control the latter.

"Which view do you want to look at first?" Sadie asked, as Levi pulled her towards him, resting his hands at her hips.

"This one," Levi said, with a mischievous grin.

"Levi, you get to look at this one all the time!" Sadie giggled, wrapping her arms around his neck and planting a kiss on his lips.

"And, I could look at this view every day for the rest of my life." Leading Sadie over to the view of the Manhattan night skyline, Levi thought it was as good a time as any. He turned Sadie to face him, took her hand in his, and dropped to one knee. A tiny gasp escaped Sadie while the crowd around them grew. Her gasp then turned into a wide smile.

"Sadie, I wrote a speech. I wrote a speech and practiced it a hundred times, and now I can't remember a word." They both laughed through tear-filled eyes.

Holding her hand, he brought it to his lips and kissed the back softly. His eyes returned to hers.

"You're my best friend, Sadie."

"You're mine. I love you, Levi."

"I love you, too."

Levi paused, smiling at her, finding the right words.

"I have spent the last seven years in awe of you, in love with you and imagining all the ways that I can make you as happy as you make me. I promise to spend my life trying. Will you do me the honour of marrying me, Sadie?"

"Levi, of course, yes. Yes!" With that answer, Levi jumped to his feet, lifting Sadie in the process and kissing her senseless, as the crowd cheered.

"Levi, this was such a surprise!" Sadie squealed as she looked down at the beautiful ring.

"I asked your parents a couple of weeks ago. I pulled them aside one by one when we went up for dinner. You didn't notice?"

"No! I can't believe you did that! I'm so happy you did though, that would've meant a lot to them."

Completely oblivious to the people around them, Sadie and Levi continued to excitedly chatter about all the details, while taking turns looking down at her hand.

"The night has only started Sadie," Levi said while looking at his watch. Pulling her close to him and walking to the elevator. They went to the 86th floor, another observation deck. They walked over to an area where people were gathered listening to a saxophone player. Levi placed twenty dollars into the case in front of the musician and nodded. He smiled in return, brought the instrument to his mouth and started to play 'Into the Mystic'.

"Our song!"

"Our song," Levi repeated, placing one hand at her waist and her other hand in his to slow dance. He didn't care there were people watching them. "Are you warm enough? It's quite cool."

"I'm perfect. This is the first song we danced to...and kissed," Sadie whispered into his ear. "It was amazing."

"Then you were mad at me," Levi joked.

"Not for long..." Sadie said, pouting, and kissed him. "How did he know to play this song?"

"I have my ways," he replied, planting a kiss on her forehead. Just then fireworks shot off in the distance over the Hudson River.

Sadie stopped, mouth agape, eyes round. Levi couldn't help but laugh.

"I would love to say that I arranged that too. But that's purely coincidence." Sadie began to laugh too. What were the chances? It was magical and beautiful and perfect.

The song came to an end. Levi put another twenty in the case, patted the sax player on the shoulder to thank him and led Sadie back to the elevators.

They went back to the Four Seasons where Levi had the room decorated with Sadie's favourite large country roses and rose petals. On a tray was champagne and room service.

"Levi!"

"Would have been a bummer if you had said no," Levi joked.

"You knew I was a sure thing!" Sadie said poking his side.

"I probably would've just gone home. I wouldn't have wanted to see this."

"It's so beautiful! You're full of surprises tonight!" Sadie squealed.

"And the night is still young," he said, winking.

Chapter 18

Piper Dinner Party

Piper had messaged Ally about a dinner party at her place. She was a great host, always throwing fab parties. She had been to a few with Levi and Sadie over the years.

Ally had spent the day with her mom at the store, putting paper up on the windows and setting up shelves, and was going to go back in the morning. Her mom was headed out with Jones. Sadie and Levi were still away and Samantha was in Hollywood. Piper was her friend too, but she usually attended her parties with the others. It would be different, especially since it was a dinner party.

Ally wore her hair down and natural as usual. She applied the tiniest amount of makeup and put on grey skinny jeans with a sheer black blouse. Ally added a long rose-gold chain with a feather pendant and a chunky rose-gold ring.

"Not sure what time I'll be home. Going to Piper's for dinner," Ally said to her mom, who was sitting at the kitchen table reading a magazine.

"Have fun," her mom said, as she got up and gave her daughter a quick hug. "Jones is taking me down to Queen's Quay tonight. Some restaurant a friend of his owns that has a nice view of the lake."

"Sounds amazing, Mom. Have fun. See you later." Ally kissed her cheek, grabbed a bottle of wine and the Greek salad she had made for the dinner, and headed to Piper's.

"Good evening, Miss Ally," Jones said. It made her smile. She was so happy that he and her mom had started dating. Two of the nicest people on the planet. "Can I call you a cab or uber?"

"Either would be fine please, Jones. I'm headed down to The Beaches tonight to a friend's on Lee Avenue. I'll be enjoying this bottle of wine, so needless to say, I won't be driving home."

"You have a great time. You deserve it with all that work you have been doing on your store."

"Thanks, Jones. I still have lots to do."

"Looks like a cab was nearby, one just pulled up."

Ally said goodbye and headed to the cab, pulling a toque out of her pocket to put on her head. The night air was so crisp that it took her breath away. She gave the driver the address to Piper's, still feeling slightly nervous about not knowing anyone there besides the host.

Ringing the doorbell, Ally could hear Jacksoul coming from the stereo and see guests standing around the kitchen island. Piper came bouncing to the door, curls flying and looking as beautiful as ever.

"Ally! So glad you came!" Piper practically pulled her inside and engulfed her in a hug all at the same time. Her vivacious personality was like a magnet, making Ally smile. *I don't know why I was nervous*, Ally thought to herself.

"Can you smell the oils you made me, Ally? Jasmine and orange!"

"You smell amazing!"

"Come, I want you to meet everyone. Sorry that Levi and Sadie couldn't make it. Those lovebirds. Oh, you know someone who's here! Wait until you see. He told me you guys used to date, wow girl, you know how to pick the hotties!" Ally was trying to keep up with Piper who was talking a mile a minute. Pulling off her toque while handing Piper her coat, she walked into the kitchen. Who she saw standing in front of her, hit her like a punch in the stomach.

Samantha never gave Nate her number and her mom sure didn't. It made sense now. Piper did. Piper didn't know the history. Piper didn't know that the sheer sight of Nate right now was making her physically ill. How the heck did they know each other, anyway?

"Hi again, Ally. It's great to see you." Nate said, walking over to Ally, holding his hand out.

Not wanting to be rude in front of Piper's guests, Ally took his hand and shook it. A little exaggerated and dropping it quickly, Ally then ran her hands down her static ridden hair. "Hi again, Nate." He looked at his hand and back at her, a smile at the corner of his mouth, but confusion in his eyes.

Piper went on to introduce the other guests, including her date, Diego. She then made Ally a drink. Ally made a mental note to tell Sadie and Samantha how hot Diego was, and then turned to see Nate still staring at her. Deciding to play along for the sake of the dinner party, and since no one was paying attention to her anymore, Ally turned to

Nate and asked, "So, what brings you back in town?"

"I wrote a book. Piper's publishing it for me."

"Of course she is…" Ally said under her breath.

"What was that?" Nate asked.

"I see."

"I had a meeting with Piper and we got talking about people we knew in Toronto. Obviously your name came up."

"I see, obviously."

"Yes, I mentioned your name and Piper said she knew you and gave me your cell and told me about your store. She was pretty excited that I was an old friend of yours."

"Old friend…" Ally repeated.

"I didn't think you would mind. Until you didn't respond to my messages, and you didn't appear too happy to see me at your store."

"Old friend," Ally repeated again, taking a large gulp of the drink Piper had since handed her. The spices of the Bloody Caesar went through her nostrils and brought tears to her eyes. She tried to gasp for air without drawing attention to herself.

She also wanted to gulp a glass of milk and splash water up her nose, but she refrained. Instead she moved closer towards the other guests, making eye contact to engage in their conversation. Nate watched her with disbelief and curiosity. Why was she being so standoffish? Most women would love to get phone calls and texts from him. Most women would have been all over him when he brought them flowers, like he had at her store. She was cold as ice, and it intrigued him. He was going to figure out why.

"Mia does some commercial photography, Ally. You should think of her when you do your website or any promotional material. She's amazing!" Piper said of her stunning friend. Ally had heard of Mia Monroe when Sadie had had some head shots done.

"We should talk, Mia. I've been procrastinating and should get on it."

"I would love to help you, Ally. Give me a shout Monday. I'm headed to Lisbon for a couple of weeks. We'll set something up before I go."

"That sounds perfect."

Why wasn't Nate all over Mia? She was stunning. Perfect pale complexion, light brown hair with natural, ombre, golden highlights that she wore in a choppy style, which she pulled off beautifully. She wore a ripped jean shirt with a tattered white t-shirt and black leather pants and looked impeccable. Silver bangles were at her wrist and a black choker at her neck. She had barely any makeup on. Her grey blue eyes were framed with long thick eyelashes and her lips a soft pink. Heck, Ally was crushing on her.

Ally turned towards Nate who was still staring at her.

"Come everyone, let's sit down for dinner, it's ready," Piper called, as she carried dishes of pasta, vegetables, and bread into the dining room. Ally went to the far side of the table, hoping someone, anyone other than Nate would sit beside her. She was fortunate; another guest named Bobby who worked with Piper sat down. Chris was hilarious and Ally realized she had met him at some of Sadie's parties with his partner. Before long he had her in stitches. It kept her busy and her mind off of her handsome ex sitting across from her watching her every move. She could feel her skin blushing from time to time, especially when he acted like no one else in the room existed. She felt like his dark eyes were penetrating her.

"Ally are you seeing anyone right now?" Nate asked her, causing the table of guests to go quiet and turn to her for the answer. He was tapping the side of his glass with his fingertips. Distracting. His perfect teeth were set in a wide smile.

"No, I'm not," Ally said to him with a smirk on her face, looking him directly in the eye. No doubt he already knew the answer to that question.

"Excellent, you'll have dinner with me tomorrow night?" Verbally it was demanding, but he added just enough inflection at the end of the sentence to turn it into a question. The guests watched for her to answer. Ally couldn't believe he was really that smug to ask in front of everyone.

Piper, sensing that Ally was none too impressed, made light of the moment. "We would all love to have dinner with you Nate. Thanks for asking. Where are we going?"

The table laughed, including Nate, and yet still didn't take his eyes off of Ally.

She did her best to ignore him and Chris made it relatively easy, telling her story after hilarious story. After dinner, Ally was helping Piper with dishes in the kitchen when Piper quietly asked her what was up with Nate.

"I had no idea he was so smitten, and he's kind of demanding, right? I would never have shared your number or how to get in touch with you if I knew there was that kind of history there. At least not without talking to you first. I'm so sorry."

"Don't worry about it, Piper. Not many know what happened. And I know that he led you to believe we were just old friends."

"Still... I'm so sorry, girl."

"We were together, but, in the end I thought it was more serious than it was. I was heartbroken. He left me for an actress."

"Ouch"

"Yet, here he is acting all interested, like nothing ever happened. I was crushed. Two years have passed. I'm not over Oliver, but, I want Oliver back. I don't need to go down this path again. Yet, I feel like I could lose myself there again if I'm not careful. You know?" Ally said looking up at Piper with tear filled eyes.

Piper pulled her in for a hug and reassured her. "I get it. You're human. I'd say go have some fun...but not if there's that kind of past there. No one wants to be hurt again."

"I fear that somehow Nate returning made me mess things up with Oliver, subconsciously."

"Seems to me you need to get to Oliver, and get him back."

"I'm trying." Ally shrugged and moved towards the dishwasher.

"No, no, I'll do these later," Piper said, taking the dishes out of her hands.

"Do you mind if I slip out?"

"I'll call you a cab."

Although Ally was disappointed that she wasn't able to say goodnight to some of the guests like Mia and Chris, Piper told her she would tell the guests that she wasn't feeling well. She knew this was one of the best moves she had made lately; she had to get out of there before she did anything she would regret.

Chapter 19

Premiere

They flew into Palm Springs a couple of days prior to the premiere. Levi and Sadie had their own room and Ally was crashing with Samantha. She thought Sam would want to spend time with Adam, but Sam wouldn't take no for an answer. Levi picked up a rental car and met them out front.

The sun was blinding and the hot air hit them like a wall as they exited the airport. There were so many limos and extravagant cars all pulled up in front of the building. Ally knew that the place was crawling with movie stars with the film festival underway. Flouncy summer hats, summer scarves, and Ray Bans camouflaged celebrity appearances. It was clear that there were stars everywhere because as many people as there were, there was security personnel everywhere.

The plan was to take in some sun and relaxation ahead of the premiere of Sam's new movie. Everyone knew Ally needed it, even though there was so much work to do before the grand opening of the store.

Levi interrupted Ally's thoughts, jumping out of the car and running around to the passenger side to open the doors for Sadie and Ally. Levi then picked up the luggage and put it in the trunk for them. You would think they were famous, the way he treated them. Sadie had hit the jackpot with this one, and now they were engaged. Ally couldn't have been happier for them. Sadie rested her hand on the back of Levi's seat and turned to tell him the hotel they were going to.

Ally couldn't help but admire the beautiful rock on Sadie's finger. It was a 3 karat pink, emerald-cut diamond on a platinum band wrapped in diamonds. It was magnificent. Levi had had it custom made for Sadie. She also couldn't help but feel a little green with envy.

"We're here. Are we supposed to call for Samantha?" Levi asked, as he pulled up to the valet. Doormen were already opening their doors as Levi was getting the luggage out of the back and putting it on a trolley. The concierge followed them in to find out their rooms and then went to deposit the luggage. Ally hadn't stayed in a hotel since the amazing time they had had in London and Paris. She just couldn't stop thinking of Oliver at every turn.

It was no surprise that they were completely star struck. Ally and Sadie had met some pretty cool people before, Adam Lane included. But tonight seemed to be a whole new caliber of people. Samantha had risen to success by Canadian standards years before, appearing in many Canadian television shows and indie productions. Her star status went worldwide when she starred in her last movie, a Hollywood blockbuster. Now everyone wanted her. Her friends were thrilled for her.

Ally couldn't wait to see the movie! Ally, Piper, Diego, Sadie, and Levi sat beside Samantha and Adam in a VIP section of the theatre. They had heard great things about the drama. Samantha had been all over the tabloids recently, mostly for the movie, but also for her relationship with Adam. Ever since Samantha brought Adam to the party she threw when Sadie finished the last book, people were so interested. For the first time, Ally was starting to think that it was all for show. It wasn't unheard of for stars to be asked to pretend to be in a relationship for the purpose of promotion.

There were new rumors swirling that Adam was seen with another actress. Ally hoped the rumours were false or that Samantha was at least in on the rouse. Samantha had been through her own heartache and had been trying to avoid dating at all costs.

Ally thought about Oliver. He would have really enjoyed this, having been a fan of many in the room. He would have been there beside her, impeccably dressed, and holding her hand. She missed him so.

Ally pinched herself daily at the fact that some of her closest friends were such big successes. Samantha, a movie star, and Sadie, a successful author. Sadie had just been contacted about a movie deal with one of her books. Levi was sorting out the details, but there was talk that Samantha might be the lead actress.

Ally now knew that success was measured by how happy you were. She knew that opening the store was her dream and she couldn't wait. She believed in her products and knew others would soon too. Her measurement of success was not based on stardom or money. She measured her success by her own happiness; having her store and making oils made her happy.

The room went dark and everyone went silent, waiting for the movie to start. 'The song Love is a Losing Game' by the late Amy Winehouse began to play. She felt someone looking at her in the dark, and looked to her right. Nate was leaning forward on his knees, his chin resting on his folded hands. He lifted two fingers to signal a hello and smiled wickedly. He then sat back, out of view.

Geez, stalk much? She had to admit, he was gorgeous though. That smile. He was wearing a suit, with his black hair slicked back and clean shaven. Like a fifties advertising man.

Her phone lit up on her lap. She was thanking herself for turning off the ringer earlier.

"Meet up later?" Nate asked her.

Could she even consider going down that road again? It would definitely be a rebound. She missed Oliver terribly. She knew that although it might be fun and a distraction, she was also smart enough to know that she would be at risk of falling for Nate all over again, and she would lose any chance of ever getting back together with Oliver. Upon hearing her with Nate, Oliver would put the nail in the relationship coffin. Nate was nothing more than eye candy, a smooth actor, and there would be other 'Sashas', she was sure of it.

Can't. Take care Nate, she responded. Ally turned off her phone and put it into her clutch.

Chapter 20

Final Straw

After the movie they headed to the restaurant and after party.

Nate slipped into the empty seat right beside Ally.

"What is your problem?" she boldly asked.

"I could ask the same of you," he said, with one eyebrow raised.

Turning to look him directly in the eye, Ally firmly said, "I'm not interested, Nate. Haven't I made that pretty clear?"

Leaning in close he said, "You've said that, but I don't believe you."

"Let me make it clear now. I have no interest in you." Ally knew the only way to deal with someone like Nate was to be direct.

"Ouch," he said with a laugh. Ally knew he wasn't used to hearing this. "Come on, Ally." Nate reached out his hand and placed it on hers. She quickly pulled her hand away and placed it on her lap. At the same time, she could have sworn she saw a flash. She hadn't noticed any photographers, hopefully it was someone taking a selfie. If this encounter ended up in a magazine and Oliver saw it, it would foil any attempts at getting him back. Oliver would be devastated.

"I'm done trying to be nice, Nate. I'm not interested, nor will I ever be."

"Ally-cat, we had something special." Using the affectionate nickname he used to call her made her cringe. "I was hoping we could reconnect since I'm back in Toronto for a while," he said, while looking into her eyes, his hand now coming to rest on top of her thigh. *Man he had nerve after busting her heart into a million pieces!* Ally looked up to see Sadie looking at her with concern.

"For starters, you made it pretty clear that I wasn't all that special, to you," Ally responded.

"Why? How?" Nate asked, surprised. "Is this about Sasha? Let's talk about that."

"Of course it's about Sasha...and I'd rather not." His close proximity was unnerving in a bad way. Feelings boiled up inside of her. She was having anxiety over being in a situation that she didn't want to be in and feeling cornered.

"For the record, I fled because I was crazy about you. I still am," he started to explain. "As soon as Piper told me she knew you, I thought, what better way to reconnect."

"Yes, you sure showed me you were crazy, by leaving me, heartbroken," Ally said, standing up.

"Ally-cat, let me explain, she meant nothing."

Ally rolled her eyes and said, "And, you mean nothing to me. Goodbye Nate. She turned on her heel and left him to watch her walk away. She went to the restroom to pull herself together. *Sasha had meant nothing? Wanted to reconnect? He was delusional.* Tears burned her eyes, but like hell she was going to let him make her cry. She had vowed to herself that wouldn't happen ever again. *I'm keeping this promise to myself, dammit.*

"What was that all about?" Sadie asked Ally as she entered the washroom, having watched Ally head there.

"Nate. He can't take no for an answer."

"And you're not interested?" Samantha confirmed from behind Sadie as she also entered the ladies room. Ally shook her head no. "What a jerk! Don't cry hun, he's not worth it."

"No, he isn't. I'm not even that upset about him. It's Oliver. I need to see him in person. I need to explain that I've made a big mistake. AND now I'm worried the paparazzi got a photo of us talking in there. I saw a flash. If Oliver saw that he would be so mad."

"Well, all I can ask is, what are you doing here?" Samantha asked.

"Here?" Ally asked, confused by Samantha's question.

"Yes, it seems to me you should be somewhere else, talking in person with Oliver."

Ally's eyes lit up with an idea sparked by Samantha's comment.

"It seems that you know what you need to do," Sadie said, "And we will support you anyway we can."

"I have to go," Ally announced, beaming. "I have to go to London."

Ally kissed her friends on the cheeks and gave them hugs before running to catch a cab, first to the hotel, then back to the airport to go home to Canada, and then to London. It was going to take at least a couple of days to get there and she was prepared to do whatever it took.

The girls headed back out to the tables where Levi was waiting.

"Everyone went outside for fresh air," Levi explained, gesturing at the empty table.

"Do you want me to come with you?" Sadie called after Ally.

"No, I need to do this alone," Ally answered, smiling, and running out the door to get a cab.

"What did I miss?" Levi whispered to Sadie.

"Ally's going to London to talk to Oliver," Sadie proudly told Levi. "Don't warn him," she said, pointing at Levi.

Holding his hands up, Levi responded, "Wouldn't dare. That's awesome. He'll be surprised I'm sure. He's been so bent up about it all."

"He hasn't answered any of her calls or texts since that night."

"I can't see why, he's not the type to just ignore someone."

"I hope it all works out," they said at the same time, and then looked at each other, smiling.

Chapter 21

London Calling

She wasn't sure exactly what she was going to say. She was terrified she would be too late and Oliver would've already moved on. It had been a month and not a lot of time, but certainly enough time to find someone else. *What if he found the woman of his dreams?* What if she came all this way and he refused to see her? Could he be that angry? What if he was back with his ex-girlfriend Hilary, the one that had drooled all over him when they were in London a couple of months ago?

Ally's stomach churned as the airplane landed and came to a halt. Some passengers were nauseous from flying. Ally was also a bundle of nerves. When she exited the plane she went straight to a washroom and threw up. Thankfully she had only brought carry on and didn't need to worry about her luggage.

Coming out of the bathroom stall Ally looked in the mirror. She looked tired and sad. Finding a dry spot on the counter, Ally dropped her two bags down and splashed some water on her face. She then dug through her bag for some gum. "This will do until I get to the hotel to brush my teeth," she said aloud to herself.

Exiting the washroom, Ally pulled out her cell phone and found Wi-Fi in the airport. She then messaged her mom and Sadie.

I made it. Sadie wrote.

Thanks for letting me know, love you xo, her mom responded.

Here for you, anytime. Day or night, call me. Keep me posted. Sadie answered.

Ally headed to her hotel, knowing that Oliver would be off work soon. She wanted to freshen up and change. Her stomach was still doing acrobats moves. She thought she knew exactly what she would do once she was here, but now, she wasn't so sure.

Dropping her things on her bed she checked her watch again. It was 4:30 local time. She knew he would be working until close to six. She wanted to be waiting in the lobby of his office building. Just in case his timing was different tonight than usual, Ally hurried so that she could catch a cab over there.

Applying only concealer, mascara and lip balm, Ally used her fingers and a little hair serum to tame her wild auburn tresses. She was wearing a black turtleneck, with skinny dark wash jeans and black, high-heeled ankle boots. She grabbed her black mid-length trench, her tan-coloured Michael Kors bag, and headed out.

"It's now or never," Ally said aloud to herself.

The cab pulled up in front of Oliver's investment firm. Ally paid the driver and headed into the foyer of the building. There were dark leather couches flanked by green plants in high cream coloured pots. She sat down, crossing her legs, clutching her bag to her chest.

Security walked past, smiled and said hello, asking if they could help her. "No thank you, just waiting for someone," Ally replied.

Each time the elevator rang and opened, she jumped out of her skin. Her empty stomach growled with a reminder that she not only hadn't eaten yet, but the she also had cleared out anything that was in her stomach at the airport. With shaking hands she opened her water and drank some to fill the void for now. Spilling water on herself in the process, Ally felt like a nervous wreck.

Finally the elevator opened and Oliver exited. He looked so good that her breath caught in her throat. How she missed him. He was so handsome in his navy, tailored suit with pinstripe shirt and whimsical tie. Knowing him, his socks were probably a fun design as well. His hair had been cut since she saw him last and he was clean shaven today. How she wanted to run her fingers along his strong jaw line. Lay kisses upon that mouth she missed so much. Tell him how sorry she was. She jumped to her feet, her short stature still hidden by the tall plants.

A loud laugh followed him out of the elevator. Ally froze. Hilary stepped out of the lift and bounced to his side, enjoying some playful banter.

What the hell was SHE doing here? What was SHE laughing at? Did SHE just touch his arm? They were headed straight towards her, but couldn't see her for the plants. Oliver leaned in close and said something in her ear, causing her to laugh even more and squeeze his upper arm.

Her worst fear was coming true. She had come all this way for nothing. He had moved on, and he had moved on with the beautiful Amazon woman. Her heart was breaking in a million pieces.

This was her moment to stand up and interject as he walked past. To ask to speak with him and profess her love.

But she panicked and as they walked past, she sat down and threw her face into her oversized bag, pretending to look for something.

She peeked her eyes out over the bag to watch their shoes pass by her, her heart beating in her throat. She thought she was going to be sick again. Her head pounded. Her heart was breaking again. She was headed back to Canada with a broken heart and her tail between her legs. Tears began to escape her eyes.

Waiting until their feet were out of view, Ally stood up. She was lightheaded from her empty stomach and pulled her water out of her bag and took another sip. She would go hail a cab, and head back to the hotel to collect her things.

"Ally?"

Her head whipped around towards the sound of his voice. He was now walking directly towards her. His long strides were at her side in seconds. She had thought it was safe to get up and that Oliver and Hilary had left the building. What she hadn't realized is that Oliver thought there was something about the woman with the red curls and he couldn't mistake the familiar scent of fresh essential oils. He looked back several times and once outside the familiar face stopped him in his tracks.

Her face flushed.

"Ally, what are you doing here?" Oliver asked.

Ally went to speak but the Amazon woman had followed him in and was now standing behind him.

"Um, I…" she stuttered looking from Oliver to Hilary and back to Oliver.

He turned to his tall colleague and said, "Hilary, I'll see you tomorrow."

"Okay," Hilary said as her eyes narrowed and peered past him at her competition, "See you tomorrow." She kissed his cheek. Oliver gave Hilary a questioning look and turned his concerned eyes back to Ally.

"What are you doing here?" he asked again softly, holding his hand towards her.

"I needed to talk to you, but, I…" Ally started and stopped, considering if he was already with Amazon woman, she didn't want to make a fool of herself. She looked down and then back up and into his eyes.

"You can talk to me, Ally," he said. "Come, I'll take us to my place." He held her hand close to his body like he always had, and motioned towards the door.

They drove in silence to his Kensington 8 home, cautiously looking at each other on the way. The neighbourhood was one of the most expensive areas in London. Sometimes Ally forgot just how affluent Oliver was. It just wasn't that important to her.

When they arrived, Oliver came around to open her door as he always had. Holding out his hand he helped her out of the car and closed the door behind her. He led her to the grand entrance, opening the heavy wooden door, and immediately turned to Ally.

He looked pensive, nervous but also there was a heat in his eyes that she recognized. Letting her bag fall to the floor, Ally leapt up into his arms, wrapping her legs around his waist. He backed her up against the door, one hand under her thigh, the other in her hair. They kissed, they kissed like lovers who hadn't seen each other in years.

Setting her down Oliver engulfed her in a warm hug.

"Ollie…"

"I've missed you, love." Oliver said in her hair.

"Ollie, it's been horrible," Ally said, sobbing into his chest.

"It has," he said pulling back to look at her. "Ally, you're quite pale. Can I get you a glass of water?"

"Yes please, I might need to bother you for a cracker. I haven't ate"

"I'll get you water and a cracker, but then, let's go for dinner. I know a nice place nearby where we can talk, catch up. Sound good?"

"How about we order in? Then we can really catch up?" Ally said winking at him.

"Chinese or pizza?" he answered without skipping a beat.

Chapter 22

Forgiveness

They spent the entire evening in each other's arms, talking well into the early morning hours. There was so much to say. They slept in, with Oliver only waking long enough to text the office that he wouldn't be in. Oliver had fell back to sleep when Ally pulled on his housecoat and tiptoed into the kitchen for a glass of water. Pouring herself a glass from the stainless steel fridge, Ally wandered into the lounge where they had spent most of the evening by dim light.

His flat was luxurious, although empty which was likely because he had just moved in. The walls were painted a calm seafoam colour with extra-large trim in off-white, large windows and beige sheer curtains. He had a chocolate brown coloured couch and chair, coffee table, but there was no television, no picture frames or art on the wall. It looked sad.

The night before Ally had apologized for the events that had led up to their break up. She went on to explain about some of the things she needed to work through and her commitment to getting the help she needed in order to make their relationship work. This included letting go of the pain of her past breakups, her feelings about her dad, and money. All her life money had appeared, but her dad didn't. To this day she didn't like to accept handouts from anyone.

Oliver apologized for his lack of sensitivity where money was concerned. He knew how important it was for her to do the store on her own. She had made her feelings about it very clear and he had downplayed that.

He also admitted that he didn't know the first thing about her relationship with her dad, and from now on he was there for her. He was heartbroken to hear how some men had treated her over the years, and vowed he would make every effort to change her opinion of men going forward. Ally even told him every detail about Nate over the last few weeks and the picture that could end up in the paper. She didn't want any surprises and he thanked her for that.

It didn't help however, that his phone was going off with texts from Hilary. At one point Ally saw the name light up on his phone.

"So, what's the deal with her? Is Hilary your girlfriend, again?" Ally bravely asked Oliver as they sat on the couch eating leftovers out of Chinese take-out containers.

"No, Hilary is not my girlfriend."

"I didn't drive you into her arms?"

"I am not interested in Hilary, or anyone else for that matter. I only want you, Ally."

"Well, I thought…"

"Ally, just because we broke up, doesn't mean I'm going to go looking for a replacement."

"Not even to get back at me out of anger?"

"Mostly because of that."

"Why is she texting you like mad?" Ally said, pointing to his phone.

"She may be interested in more, but I had a talk with her just last week. It's not going to happen. Not now, not ever."

"You work together?"

"Yes, we do."

"And that's all?"

"Yes. She's good at what she does. I have no reason to let her go because of our past history."

"No, I guess not."

"However, I have no problem telling her that texting me other than for work is inappropriate. I will deal with it, Ally. Don't give it another thought."

"Michael and I only went out for dinner a couple of times. Nothing else."

"I don't care."

"I also spoke to Nate only because he came by the store, he was at Piper's, and I ran into him at the film festival. But I told him I'm not interested in going down that path again."

"I don't care, Ally."

"Ollie…" Ally wanted to explain and she wanted him to understand. She wanted to know that he understood.

"I don't mean that I don't care that you were dating someone else, or talking to Nate. I care very much about that." He paused, adding, "It just doesn't change how I feel about you."

"But you weren't taking my calls."

"What calls?"

"After the restaurant, I called you a few times."

"Ally, I lost my phone earlier that day!"

"What?" Relief began to wash over her.

"Yes, I lost my phone sometime before the restaurant that day."

"Ollie!"

"I didn't think anyone would be trying to reach me."

"Oh, Ollie. I wanted to explain. I assumed you were refusing my calls. And my drunk texts."

"Aw, did you send me drunk texts? Now those I'd want to see," he teased.

Ally set her food down on the coffee table, took Oliver's, and set it down as well. She then climbed onto his lap, resting her head against his chest. Oliver wrapped his arms around her.

"It was all a stupid misunderstanding. I shouldn't have broken up with you to begin with. I should never have gone out with Michael."

"Shhh...Don't give it another thought. The past is the past and you're here now. How long are you here for, Ally?"

"I bought a one way ticket, but I do need to get back to prepare for the opening of the store this weekend. I still have so much to do. It's quite overwhelming."

"Do you have any help?"

"My mom is helping when she gets home from work and Sadie can help more now that she's done her tour."

"That's good."

"She'll be planning a wedding soon," Ally added, smiling.

"Yes, brilliant news, I'm thrilled for them." Oliver lifted her hand to his mouth and kissed along her knuckles. Ally took her other hand and ran it through his short thick hair, stopping at the nape of his neck and leaning in to give him a kiss.

"The question is, how long are you here for, Ollie?" she asked, pensively. Her stomach was in knots as she awaited the answer. As far as she knew, it was forever, and she couldn't bear the thought of saying goodbye, again.

"To be honest, I don't know. I just got here," Oliver said, looking into her eyes. He shrugged his shoulders and gave her a sad smile.

"I figured that," Ally said, as she got up off his lap and started to clean up.

"I'll get it all sorted out though," he said, coming up behind her. He wrapped his arms around her, leaning down to kiss her hair. "I want to be where you are, love. I just need some time to sort it out."

"I know," Ally said, pausing, and turning to face him. "I just...don't want to leave you behind."

"You're not. I'm going to be right behind you, love. Just have some calls to make."

"Are you sure you're going to be able to make this happen?"

"It's my company. Yes. It's the last thing to worry about." Pausing he added, "Now, having somewhere to live when I go back is a different story." He laughed.

"You can stay with us!"

"No, no, that's okay. Not sure I could handle two redheads, and those Irish tempers," he said jokingly, and tickled her sides making Ally laugh. How he loved to hear her laugh. It was music to his ears.

"Catriona has no temper, but I on the other hand, hmmm…"

"I can handle you, now that I know what I'm dealing with," he said, smirking.

Oliver pulled her into his chest, holding her tightly against him, and hoping to calm her anxiety. Ally ran her hand up his chest and looped it around his neck, looking up at him at the same time. His light eyes watched her through his thick lashes. Gathering her hair in his hands, he tilted her head until their lips met.

When they broke apart Ally said, "How did I get so lucky, Ollie?"

Chapter 23

Papers

Ally stayed with Oliver for the next few days. Oliver wanted her to stay longer, and although it was hard to pry herself away, she knew she had to get back to finish setting up her store and prepare for the grand opening in just a few days. She had planned for this venture her whole life and had lots of planning and organizing to do to make it perfect.

Ally landed at Pearson and moved her way through the throngs of people as she made the long trek to the pickup area for arrivals, where Sadie was waiting for her. Ally sent her a quick text to let her know that she had landed and would be out in ten minutes. She stopped for a bottle of water, parched from the long flight. Setting her handbag on the counter in front of her, she rummaged through to find her wallet.

"Sorry, always the problem with having big bag," Ally said to the clerk who was waiting patiently. The lady smiled and shrugged.

"I have time."

Ally pulled out a five dollar bill and handed it to her. The clerk took it, looking at her sideways. Ally gave a small smile. Patting her hair down and wiping under her eyes with her fingers, she wondered if she looked like a hot mess. She had already freshened up using a small mirror before getting off the plane, because she had slept on the flight.

"You," the clerk said, pointing at her and then to her right.

"Pardon?" Ally said, looking down around her body. Was there something stuck to her?

"You," The clerk said again, with more force, and pointed again at Ally and then to her right. Ally followed the finger to a magazine rack.

Ally's eyes bulged. Her cheeks burned. Her stomach sank. Front page. There it was. Crap.

Irrational thoughts began to go through her head. *If I could buy up every magazine from here to London...*

"Nope, not me," Ally said, while throwing the water and change in her bag.

Ally turned quickly on her heel and ran out of the airport. Looking left to right for Sadie's car, Ally began to panic. After such a great trip, and finally everything working out with Oliver, Ally couldn't bear the thought of everything falling apart now. It was three in the morning in England and he likely wasn't awake, but he surely would wake to his friends and family giving him this update.

Her mind broke down the pictures on the cover of the magazine, Nate Fox leaning in close to Ally's ear, his hand resting on her hand...going into her store with flowers...following her out of Piper's, which she had no idea he had done. That one in particular looked worse than it was. Someone had been tracking him. The caption read: *Nate Fox getting close with mystery redhead in Toronto.* Ugh.

Sadie beeped her horn and Ally ran to the car and jumped in.

"Am I ever glad to see you, Sadie," Ally said, leaning in for a quick side hug and knocking a magazine that sat between them. Ally picked it up to look closer at the photos and then threw it in the backseat.

"How ya' doing?" Sadie asked her empathetically.

"About 15 minutes ago I was fantastic. Oliver was amazing and we worked everything out. But now...now he's going to see this. His family and friends will see this. And then what?"

"Just explain to Oliver. Levi and I can back you up, we were there."

"I told Oliver about Nate stopping by the store and seeing him at the film festival. But these pictures...the caption."

"I know it doesn't look good."

"And Piper's? I didn't even know he was coming out of the house. What they didn't take a picture of, was me driving away in a cab, by myself!" Ally cried. "I left the dinner party early, specifically so I wouldn't get caught up in Nate's web. I thought only Piper knew I was slipping out."

"Surely Oliver will understand."

As Sadie tried to comfort her best friend, Ally feverishly texted Oliver on the new cell number he had given her. She also sent private messages through every social media account he had. She hated feeling so desperate, but she was. She was desperate for him to hear it from her first.

Sadie exited highway 427 and merged onto the Gardiner. Ally's phone rang, causing her to jump mid text.

"Hello, Ollie," Ally gasped.

"Hi," he said quietly.

"Ollie, I want to explain, before other people reach you."

"I've already had a few send me screenshots of the magazine, Ally." She didn't like his change of tone.

"Can I explain?"

"Tomorrow, Ally. I'm in bed."

"Just give me second, Oliver.'

"Tomorrow."

Gulping out an okay while holding back tears, Ally knew in her heart that he was upset. She could hardly blame him. The pictures did not do her case any justice. Although she had told him about the store and film festival, she had left out some of the details like Piper's dinner and the flowers.

Hanging up the phone Ally said more curse words than Sadie even knew existed. She yelled and screamed all the way to the condo. Part crying, part laughing, mostly hysterical. Sadie tried desperately to calm her down before getting to the condo.

"I don't want to go home. I can't face my mom right now."

"You can stay with me."

"After."

"After?" Sadie asked.

"The closest pub. Now."

"You got it." Sadie exited the Gardner at York St and headed north to Wellington. She made a right and headed to a favourite spot. Once parked, they went in and ordered a round of shots and drafts. They stayed there until closing time and took a cab to Sadie's condo. Giggling, they made their way up to Sadie's and into the kitchen to have something to eat.

"We should get some sleep so that you can call Oliver in the morning," Sadie suggested.

"No."

"What do you mean, no?"

"He needs to call me. He sounded angry, I did nothing wrong."

"He was sleeping."

"He wasn't sleeping yet. He was awake. He chose not to talk to me and I'm choosing not talk to him."

"Keep it in perspective, Ally. He probably just needed time to cool off. And, think if it were reversed." There was no talking to Ally after a few drinks.

"I've got to think about that all the time, he works with his ex-girlfriend!"

"But it's not splashed on magazines for the world to see."

"Ack, whatever."

"You're so stubborn!" Sadie said, swatting her as she passed her to go to her bedroom. "Well, I'm going to bed, goodnight!"

"I'm not stubborn." Ally said to herself giggling.

She sent Oliver a text, knowing with the time change he would be up.

We just had two amazing weeks. If you're going to throw things away because of stupid pictures and words that are meant for people to buy magazines. Then, goodbye!

Ally turned her phone off and threw it in her bag, not even waiting for a reply. She then stumbled into the spare room and slept until noon.

Chapter 24

Stubborn

Ally could hear voices. She rubbed her scratchy eyes with the back of her hand and squinted around the room. It took her a moment to figure out where she was, until the familiarity of her bedroom at Sadie's made sense. She put the pieces together of the last 24 hours. Leaving London as happy as a clam, being devastated by the magazine, and then being downright obliterated mere hours ago. She had no idea what time it was, but knew she had to get over to the store; the grand opening was tomorrow!

She heard the gentle click of the door handle and peeked above the covers to see Sadie peeking back.

"Hi, I hope we didn't wake you," Sadie said, as she sat down on the side of the bed. "How are you feeling?" Sadie crinkled her nose figuring the answer was not going to be good.

"Could be worse, could be better," Ally said, rolling onto her side, the blankets tucked under her chin. *How did Sadie look so good already? What time did she get up? She was just as inebriated as me last night...we went to the bed at the same time. So not fair.*

"Levi's here. He said Oliver is trying to reach you."

Ally rolled back and pulled the covers over her head, now remembering the last thing she did before going to sleep. A drunk text. A goodbye. *Why did people allow me to drink, much less own a phone?*

"Do you want me to get your phone?" Sadie asked.

"No, not yet," Ally answered dryly and then added, "I'll call him soon. I need to get my world together." She then rolled away to face the wall. Sadie patted her back gently.

"Okay, buddy. I'll leave you to do that." Sadie gently closed the door behind her and went back into the living room to join Levi.

Throwing the blankets off and to the side in a huff, Ally kicked her legs and pounded the bed with her fists dramatically, like a child having a temper tantrum. *Why did it always have to be so complicated? Aren't I allowed to find happiness with someone too? At least for five minutes? Stupid Nate. Stupid paparazzi. Stupid magazines.*

Ally got out of bed slowly, her head pounding. *Seems like a regular occurrence these days,* she admitted to herself. She threw on a pair of sweatpants sitting on the dresser from the last time she stayed and headed to the washroom to throw some water on her face. She had to get it together and head over to the store.

She didn't know how to feel about Oliver trying to reach her. At first she felt relief. Relief was then overshadowed by an ache in the pit of her stomach. He might be calling to end it for good, tired of the drama once and for all. She resided in the fact that she couldn't talk to him just yet. She couldn't deal with him breaking up with her and having to face everyone at the grand opening of the store the next day.

"I'm going to throw my phone out the window if he calls back again. He's driving me crazy," Levi said to Sadie, his mouth twisted. Sadie shrugged her shoulders.

"She's hungover and just waking up. Let's give her a second."

Levi's phone rang again. His eyes bulged.

"Yes, Oliver. Yes, I'm here, yes, she's here." Sadie chuckled at the expression on Levi's face. Ally was taking her time in the washroom.

"Give me the phone, Levi," Sadie demanded.

"Hi Oliver, yes, she's only just waking up. We had a late night." Sadie didn't say anything for a few minutes, instead just listened to Oliver. Finally she answered. "Yes, sounds like a plan. I will. Yes, I'll make sure of it. Bye."

Sadie whispered into Levi's ear so that Ally wouldn't hear.

"Really?" Levi asked, his eyebrow raised and a grin on his face. Sadie confirmed with a nod.

The shower started. Best place for Ally right now was to get herself together. There was a lot to do to get the store ready for tomorrow afternoon. Sadie got a coffee and a smoothie ready for Ally, packed waters and snacks for the day.

***

Sadie went with Ally to work at the store, Levi had some meetings to attend and then would bring the girls dinner. Catriona and Jones were also planning to go by later to help.

"So, did you end up calling him?"

"Who?" Ally asked oblivious.

"Um, Oliver? Who else?"

"No, not yet."

"Why?"

"I don't know."

"Are you sure?"

"I'm just not ready to have another heavy conversation with him."

"You don't even know if it will be."

"Did he say anything to you guys?"

Sadie shifted her body so that she her face wasn't in view of Ally. She was terrible with secrets and lying. Sadie wore her heart and soul on her sleeve. She remembered back to London when Oliver told Sadie and Levi he had plans to surprise Ally and take her to Paris. It killed Sadie not to grab her friend by the hands, spin in a circle squealing, and jump up and down. Levi had to coach her to be quiet the whole time. Good thing he was so good-looking and persuasive.

"Nope, just wanted to talk to you."

"Well, I'm waiting until Sunday. I have to get through tomorrow."

"Yes."

"I have a lot of people coming, I don't want to be emotional."

"I understand." Sadie felt for her bestest. She could see that Ally was likely going to be emotional regardless. Her mind was obviously elsewhere. She grabbed the same bottle and put it back more than a few times, forgetting what she went to the cupboard for. She had dropped a glass jar and spilled product all over the counter. When she dropped the latest rollerball, Sadie suggested they take a break.

"NO! I'm fine," Ally said. *Stubborn woman,* Sadie thought to herself.

"Fine," Sadie said, staying calm, knowing that Ally was having a hard time, and not to take it personally.

They worked away quietly, all afternoon. Ally barked orders, and then followed it up with apologies and hugs. She knew she was being unfair to Sadie. She just couldn't help herself.

Before long others were there to share in the work and the mood. Levi brought in soup, salads, and sandwiches from a local deli, while Catriona and Jones brought in coffee and tea. They knew adding alcohol to the mix tonight was not a good idea. They took a short break, ate, and then followed instructions. The goal was to get the place ready for party set up tomorrow. Ally was opening the doors in the afternoon, so there was a little time in the morning.

Catriona pulled Sadie aside at one point. "Is she okay?"

"She's going to be just fine," Sadie replied.

If you had asked Ally, she may have given a different answer. But no one dared. At 1:00 am Ally gave the all clear to pack up. Everyone was happy with what they had accomplished, including Ally. She said a heartfelt thank you to her friends and family and went home with her mom to go straight to bed and rest for the big day.

Chapter 25

Grand Opening

Grand opening day. It's really happening. Ally couldn't believe it was here. *I own my own store! My very own store!* It had been a dream of hers for most of her life. Some people dreamed of their wedding day or travelling the world. Ally dreamed of having her own store. A place to share her gifts, a place to be creative and a place to call her own.

Ally bounced out of bed and went straight to the shower to get ready for the day. She was grateful for a good sleep. She must have been emotionally and physically drained from the day before.

Before leaving London, she thought that her relationship with Oliver was going to be great. Maybe there would be a wedding one day. She had wanted him to be home celebrating this big milestone alongside her, but she understood that after everything, she wasn't about to rush him or complain. Oliver needed time to sort out his company and arrange working back in Toronto. Once back, he needed to find a place to live, as he had already rented out his home. It could take months. Would he halt all this planning now? Now that the magazine had published photos of her and Nate?

Hopefully one day she would be given the opportunity to explain the magazine cover to him. She had made some silly mistakes along the way in their relationship and most of it came down to a lack of communication. One thing she was sure of, was that she loved him dearly, and as hard as she tried to consider moving on without him, she simply couldn't. However, today was not that day. Today was the day her dream of owning a store was becoming a reality.

The condo was quiet. Not wanting to wake her mom after their very late night, Ally tiptoed around the condo getting ready. Although she was going to the store early, she wasn't expecting anyone to join her until the afternoon. Going into the kitchen to make coffee, Ally was surprised to find a card addressed to her sitting against the coffee maker. Opening it, a smile spread across her face and happy tears filled her eyes. It was a sweet, encouraging, and celebratory note from her mom. It was then that she knew it was going to be a great day.

Ally placed the card in the pocket of her housecoat. It was going to come with her to the store. She owed so much to her mom. Catriona's faith and support over the years was unwavering with everything she did. Catriona was a strong woman, raising Ally on her own. Her mom made her who she was today. Their bond and connection was something that could never be broken, and that, she would always treasure.

***

Ally puttered around, applying finishing touches as she sang along to the music coming from the store's Bluetooth speakers. She had a great playlist for today. Songs filled with inspiration, love and just plain fun. The caterer was putting out artisan cheese boards, mixed olive platters, and specialty breads and dipping oils. Bunches of green and red grapes were displayed amongst the yummy displays of food.

"Ally, it smells amazing in here!" Sadie exclaimed, not speaking about the food, but the essential oils, as she entered the unlocked front door. "And it looks fantastic!" She looked around at the serene seafoam green colour of the walls, whitewash stain on the wood shelving, anchored by large plain wood workspaces. The store had the original wide plank pine floors. The windows were large and bright with sheer white curtains hanging and held open with polished silver and glass tiebacks. Silver and glass chandeliers hung from the ceiling that still had the original tin tiles. The store was stunning.

The essential oils were packaged in clear glass with a silver and seafoam label. A large contrast from the original plan of dark blue glass and lime packaging. The change was a good one. Between the smells and the sights, the space captured a feeling of bliss and calm.

"I can understand why you love to be here! I would never leave!" Sadie said with excitement, handing her best friend a huge bouquet of yellow tulips.

"These are beautiful, Sadie!" Ally said, hugging her.

Ally got a large crystal vase from the back room and placed the tulips in some water. She placed the vase on the centre block island beside a display of soaps and sprays. She then looked to find Sadie picking up a rollerball from the shelf and squeal.

"The Sadie! I got my own scent! This is awesome!" Sadie laughed and hugged Ally. "What a great idea!" Sadie went on to smell the different scents named after their friends. She then walked around to find bath products, products to help with minor health ailments like headaches or tummy issues, and lastly, even cleaning supplies.

"This place is amazing! I hope you're ready! I plan on getting quite a few things. Everyone will."

"Just take what you want, silly," Ally replied, beaming. "But, yes, I'm ready."

Levi came in next. Ally wondered why they hadn't arrived at the same time.

"Was it difficult to find parking?" Ally asked him.

"No, not at all. I had to run a quick errand." He walked over to Ally and gave her a big hug and a kiss on the cheek. "Congratulations! It looks amazing!" he said, looking around. They both had been there last night, but there was something special, about walking in this morning with Ally's final touches applied.

Levi winked and smiled at his fiancée, who responded with a huge grin.

Soon Catriona, Jones, Samantha, Piper, and more had all arrived. The store was buzzing, the music was playing, everyone was enjoying the food and wine, smelling samples, and enjoying the company. Ally had a nice surprise for everyone; a swag bag full of goodies from the store. She couldn't wait to hand them out.

Piper's friend Mia Munroe had arrived to photograph the event, along with the mayor for the ribbon cutting. At the same time, Sadie came over to Ally with another bouquet of flowers, this time tulips, roses and lilies, all in white. "What are these for?" Ally looked at her, puzzled.

"Not from me," Sadie said, and moved to the side. There, at the front of the store, holding red ribbon and scissors for the cutting ceremony, was Oliver.

Letting out a gasp, Ally pushed past Sadie and flew into Oliver's arms.

"I wouldn't miss this, love," he said, kissing the top of her head.

Ally hugged him tight, her arms wrapped around his body, buried into his chest.

"I'm sorry I didn't call back. I was afraid."

"Don't be. Please. Never with me."

"Ollie…I need to explain."

"If you need to explain, I'm all ears - tomorrow. Today, is your day. Let's celebrate," Oliver said, stepping back and waving the ribbons and scissors he was still holding.

"Let's celebrate" Ally said, stepping up on her tiptoes to lay a long slow kiss on Oliver's lips. She then called her family and friends over for the ceremony.

They lined the sidewalk outside at the store, the red ribbon stretching from end to end. Ally stood in the centre with the mayor, her mom, Sadie, and Oliver all gathered around. On the count of three, Ally snipped the ribbon and the crowd let out a cheer. Mia had captured it all on film.

It was the happiest day of her life.

Chapter 26

Settling In

The grand opening was amazing and Ally was on an all-time high. She couldn't remember another time feeling this happy. There was nothing or no one that could take away the euphoria she was feeling or wipe the smile from her face. The doors of her store were officially opened to the public. The turnout was huge, the sales were fantastic and her man was back.

To say it was a surprise seeing Oliver there yesterday was an understatement. She didn't know when they would talk again, let alone see each other. Oliver was thoughtful and romantic; he knew how important the grand opening was to Ally. Oliver also knew what the papers and paparazzi's could be like; they were ruthless in the United Kingdom. He merely couldn't talk that night about it until he cooled off a little. He still didn't like seeing her with Nate. He didn't know what the story was behind one of the three photos and he needed clarification. He wasn't about to throw away what they had away over some photos until he knew more. He had lost her once and wasn't going to let that happen again.

Ally had explained each picture in great detail. Oliver didn't need to hear anymore; he had wrapped her in his arms and promised next time to not let fear or anger determine when it was a good time to communicate. They knew they were far from perfect at this relationship gig and promised that they would always keep working at it and never give up on each other.

Oliver had brought only a handful of things with him on this spontaneous trip to surprise Ally. So it was going to be a bigger surprise when she saw that he had hired a real estate agent to help him find a home immediately. Ally admired his ability to get things done. Money was no object when he decided he needed something. The agent found a beautifully renovated older home in the Annex neighbourhood of Toronto. The home was easily worth a cool two million in the current market. Oliver didn't bat an eyelash, but wanted to make sure that Ally loved it before he signed anything.

He picked up Ally when the store closed on Monday evening and took her to see the house. She was instantly confused when he didn't take the usual route.

"Where are we going?" Ally asked.

"I want your opinion on something," Oliver said, looking at her with a mischievous grin.

"On what?"

"You'll see…it's a surprise."

"A surprise! I'm intrigued." She chattered on about her day, barely taking a breath between stories, clearly in her element with her new store. Oliver loved hearing her talk. She had a smooth and sexy tone to her voice; she also had the talent of a great storyteller, using inflections to convey the message so that you felt as though you were there.

They pulled into the driveway twenty minutes later.

"Where are we? Who lives here?" Ally asked, even more confused.

"Maybe me, that's why I need your opinion."

"Seriously!! It's stunning, Ollie!"

"I thought so, too. Shall we check it out, my love?" he said, already out of the car and opening her door while holding out his hand.

"I'd love to!" Ally squealed and squeezed his arm with her other hand.

The agent was waiting just inside the grand entrance and proceeded to give them the tour. The home was elegant, completely updated throughout and had a kitchen to die for. Ally could picture her sexy man in an apron making them dinner. The kitchen led to an outdoor paradise, where she could picture parties with their friends.

No expense was spared on this home, inside or out. If Oliver wanted to know, she would give him her honest opinion. *Buy it, buy it now, and please ask me to move in with you*, she thought to herself.

Oliver couldn't move into his other home since it had only been a few months and the lease was signed for one year with the current tenants. He liked the location of the new home as it was closer for Ally to get to her store than from her mom's or from his old place. He was hoping she might even move in with him one day. Ally was a delicate creature though, and he wasn't about to broach that subject just yet.

"What do you think?" Oliver asked.

"I love it. I really love it."

"Should I buy it?"

"YES! You'd be crazy to pass this place up!" Ally said, weaving her fingers into his. He pulled up the sleeve of his camel overcoat, looked at his watch, and debated whether to have the agent draw up the papers tonight.

"How fast do I need to act on this one, Derek?" Oliver asked the agent. He worked with him on all of his properties for personal and business.

"If you are interested, I'll draw up the papers this evening and swing by in the morning."

Oliver looked at Ally one more time, who was smiling ear to ear. She was enchanting, beautiful, and intelligent. She was stubborn, feisty, and fierce. She held his hand and his heart. Whatever she wanted, it was hers, and if she wanted this house then he was going to buy it.

"I'm interested, we're interested," Oliver said, squeezing Ally's hand, and giving her a wink. In turn, Ally leapt into his arms, leaving a trail of kisses down his cheek. Oliver laughed and said to Derek, "I'm staying at the Four Seasons. Give me a call in the morning."

Oliver drove Ally up to her mom's house, much to his chagrin. Ally said that she had promised her mom they would have breakfast in the morning as they hadn't spent much time together lately. Her mom was also going to join her at the store for the day. Ally wanted to get her trained up so that her mom could look after the store. Eventually Ally would also consider hiring a couple more people to work.

Oliver pulled up to the condo. "I'll park, and walk you up?"

"You don't have to walk me up, Ollie. But you can park for a minute, so that we can say a proper goodbye." She said, this time giving HIM a wink.

"I can do that," he responded quickly.

"I can't believe you bought a house!" she said, squealing.

"You really think I had any choice with those emerald eyes looking back at me, willing me to buy it?" Oliver replied with a kiss on her cheek.

"It was that obvious, huh?" She smiled sweetly back at him. Lifting his hand off of the gear shift, Ally placed it in her lap, interlocked her fingers with his, and placed her other hand over them.

"What's going on up there, Ally?" he asked, half worried to hear the answer.

"I love you, Oliver. And I know I haven't made it easy. I know I have my quirks and I'm not the easiest person to be with," Ally confessed.

"Hey, stop," he said, gently. He turned his body toward her and took his free hand to tilt her chin until her eyes met his. "I love you, too."

Moving her hands up around his neck, she kissed him passionately. Oliver moved his left hand to her hip.

When they finally broke apart, they were dazed, trying to catch their breath.

"No one has ever made me feel how you do, Ally," he said moving his hand up to her hair, tucking a strand behind her ear. "And you don't get to take all the credit for things being complicated." He winked and ran his thumb along her bottom lip. "I'm sure I added to that."

"Well, you do have that Amazon, beautiful ex-girlfriend who still loves you and works for you."

"Am I sensing jealousy still, Ally, after everything?" he asked playfully, not trying to start anything. He had his own jealous streak and she knew as much.

Ally playfully pouted, sticking out her bottom lip which only encouraged Oliver to nibble it, and take her into another long kiss.

"Whose idea was it for me to come home tonight?"

"I believe you were pretty adamant about it," he joked. The gentleman that he was, he got out and came around the car again to open her door. "Come, let me at least walk you up."

This time when she got out of the car she surprised him by leaping onto his back and getting a piggyback ride to the front door. They giggled like school kids, Oliver letting her down just outside of the elevator, just in time for a snobby older couple who were exiting the elevators to give their disapproving looks. Oliver ushered Ally on to the elevator as she jumped into is arms. The laughter continued up to her mom's condo and when they found a note saying that Catriona would be home early in the morning, they celebrated over a bottle wine.

Chapter 27

Samantha

"What do you think?" Sadie said, beaming.

"Oh, Sadie...it's perfect." Ally said, holding back tears.

Sadie leaned forward to kiss Ally on the cheek, and then walked over to the mirror to take a closer look. She was in love. Sadie had told the dress clerk what she wanted and she had nailed it. It draped Sadie like it was made just for her.

The fitted, ivory dress had a satin slip with an overlay of delicate tulle and lace. The dress went to the floor with a train at the back. It was bohemian, rustic, and incredibly romantic. It complimented Sadie's natural beauty.

For the fall wedding, Sadie was planning on the country roses that she loved so much in orange, red and yellow. She was planning to wear one behind her ear with her golden hair flowing to one side.

"This is it. I don't need to try anything else. I love it."

"It really is perfect for you, Sadie. If I had to picture what your dress would look like, this would be it."

"I hope Levi likes it."

"Are you kidding me? You're going to bring him to his knees."

"Oh Sadie, you look beautiful." Sadie's mom entered the room, rushing to her daughter to give her a hug. The tears began to flow for the three of them.

"I can't wait," Sadie said, giggling. She took one more walk around in the dress, and then changed to help find her mom and Ally their dresses. Samantha and Piper were also going to be in the wedding and were due to arrive any minute.

Sadie had an idea of what she wanted the girls to wear. The colour was a dark, dusty blue, almost grey, a colour which Sadie had always loved. Ultimately the dresses were their choice; she didn't even mind if they went with different styles.

The bridal shop brought out wine and hors d'oeuvres while the girls tried on dresses. They decided on a similar but simpler style than Sadie's, fitted and to the floor, in the colour Sadie loved. They complimented the bride perfectly; each woman bringing their own beauty to the wedding party. Jaws were going to drop. Ally hoped Oliver's would. They would be walking down the aisle as maid of honour and best man.

After finishing up at the dress shop the girls headed out for dinner at a new restaurant downtown. They were settled into a VIP section because dining with Samantha without drawing a crowd was becoming more challenging every day. Sadie was not as recognizable and her fans were more discreet, sliding a book in front of her and asking for a signature. Samantha's fans were wild and wanted selfies. She was gracious about it, but it could get old for her friends who were trying to have a hot meal and a visit.

"Look who just walked in!" Ally squealed.

"Who?" The girls' heads spun towards the door in unison.

"Oh, it's just Nick Stone," Samantha muttered.

"Just Nick Stone?" Piper questioned Samantha, with her eyebrows raised.

"Pretty sure anyone who is living and breathing would never say just Nick Stone," Ally countered, with a funny face. Nick Stone was one of the biggest stars in the world. He was in blockbuster hit after hit. Not one for scandals he led a pretty quiet life outside of Los Angeles and lived in New York. He was currently in Toronto filming and was rumoured to have bought a home in Yorkville, an upscale area where many stars could live without being bothered by paparazzi on a regular basis.

"He's not that big of a deal."

"Oh really?" Sadie asked. The three girls exchanged looks around Samantha.

"What?" Samantha asked.

"Nothing." Piper answered.

"You must know him to have that kind of opinion, or lack of one," Sadie said.

"Do you know Nick Stone?" Ally asked her directly.

"I've met him briefly." Samantha responded.

"Looks like he's coming this way…" Piper discreetly spoke out of the side of her mouth. She was right; Nick Stone was headed directly for their table.

"Hi Samantha, great to see you," Nick said, smiling and reaching his hand out across the table to Samantha. He was charming with his piercing, blues eyes, blond hair currently longer than usual, likely for a role. He was as tall as Oliver but easily twice the size, his muscles bulging through the material of his shirt. His hand was the size of a baseball mitt, Samantha's looking like a child's in his. The women sat with their mouths gaping open, looking from Nick to Samantha, and feeling the fireworks between the two of them.

"Hi, Nick, right?" Samantha answered nonchalantly, shaking his hand. Piper gasped and Ally started to giggle and coughed to cover it up. They were surprised by Samantha's coyness.

"Yes, Nick." His smile got bigger. Challenge was accepted. He looked around the table and introduced himself to everyone.

"Would you like to join us, Nick?' Sadie offered, much to Samantha's chagrin.

"Thank you, Sadie, but I need to get back," he explained, pointing his thumb to the group sitting across the restaurant. Samantha's expression remained stoic. "Great meeting all of you," he said looking around the table. "I hope to see you again, Samantha."

Samantha gave him a quick grin and then turned her eyes towards the menu she was holding in her hand. Nick excused himself looking slightly confused and uncomfortable and went back to his party. Several in his group looked over to their table, recognizing Samantha. Her hair style and colour changed all the time, but no one could mistake her style and her fashion model presence. Samantha's big brown eyes were complimented with high cheekbones and a breathtaking smile.

"What was that all about?" Ally asked.

"What?" Samantha asked innocently, tucking a strand of platinum hair behind her ear.

"Girl, you were cold," Piper observed.

"Well, he deserves it," Samantha said, justifying her behaviour.

"Why?" Sadie asked.

"I met him a while ago."

"What happened... dish," Ally demanded.

"It's not a big deal."

"Um, apparently it is," Sadie pointed out.

"We had great conversation. I thought everything was going good. Then this young thing with huge ta-tas and a dress the length of the shirt, walks up and pulls him by the hand away from me. He just left me standing there. Rude!" Samantha blurted all at once.

"Oh. Ouch," Piper said.

"Not a big deal, and neither is he."

"Well, maybe they came to that event together," Sadie offered.

"Then he shouldn't have been flirting with me."

"Fair, but maybe it was nothing serious with the young thing, but he couldn't just ignore her," Ally suggested.

Samantha was so down to earth and new to the Hollywood scene that she had little patience for egos, and she thought his was big.

"Whatever."

"Seems to me that you left an impression on him," Sadie said.

"Seriously, Sam, he couldn't take his eyes off of you," Piper added.

Ally looked across the room and said, "And he still hasn't."

Samantha lifted her gaze towards Nick's table and right into his eyes. Embarrassed, she shifted in her seat, turned her body towards Ally and asked her to switch seats. Ally shrugged and obliged. Ally saw Nick chuckle from across the room at the move and gave him a small smile. She had never seen Samantha act this way, not even when Ally told her about her experience with Nate Fox. All Ally could think was that Samantha had it bad for Nick.

"New topic," Samantha requested. "Let's talk wedding details. How can we help you, Sadie?"

The ladies looked around the table at each other and quickly took cue.

"I'd like to plan a girl's getaway before the wedding, somewhere warm, maybe a yoga retreat." Sadie said.

"Sounds great, I'm in. I am not working right now, so I'd love to help as much as possible." Samantha announced. *For now,* Sadie thought to herself knowing that she would soon be surprising Samantha with an offer to star in the movie based on Sadie's book "Between the Stars". She was pretty certain Samantha would say yes. She had always said if any of the books turned into movies, she was game. She hoped so; there was no one better suited to play the heroine.

"I'm pretty flexible, so let me know. Yoga retreat sounds just like what the doctor ordered." Piper added.

"Perfect, I knew you guys would love it," said Sadie.

Chapter 28

Home

Months had passed since Sadie and Levi's engagement, since Ally's grand opening, and since Oliver had back for good. They enjoyed a beautiful summer, spending time together and with their friends at Levi and Sadie's cottage, enjoying Oliver's new boat on Lake Ontario, going to concerts, and backyard parties at Piper's and Samantha's. Ally was enjoying her store and able to take time away now that she had hired a few people. Ally's relationship with Oliver had never been better.

It was Friday morning and Ally's first of several days off from the store for Sadie and Levi's wedding. There was lots to do as the maid of honour and she couldn't be happier to help. She thought she might be just as excited as if she were the bride! She looked over at a sleeping Oliver and gently lifted the covers, slipping out of bed. As she entered the living room she admired what a beautiful morning it was. The weather was supposed to be like this all weekend, which was perfect for a wedding at the lake. The sun was coming up and a streak of light covered the tops of the trees. The air felt crisp first thing in the morning but was going to warm up as the day went on. Fall colours were in full coverage and the backyard was beautiful. She imagined the lake would be breathtaking.

Oliver had asked her to move in with him last month during a romantic stroll on the waterfront. He had had an extra key made and had it put on a pewter heart keychain, placing it in her hand when they stopped to sit on a bench. It was corny and sweet and her heart burst with love at the gesture. She had been secretly hoping he would ask. She wanted to spend more time with him and take the relationship to the next level. They were always together anyway. Soon they were learning how to live together and when to give each other space. Their silly arguments usually ended with laughter and they always had fun making up.

Ally had fun adding her personal touches to their home. Her quirky bohemian style including oversized afghans for the couches, colourful ceramic dishes, and lots of plants, complimented Oliver's understated decor. Her store also made its way into their home; salt lamps, diffusers, and essential oils made the house smell amazing and gave it ambiance.

Oliver did most of the cooking because he enjoyed it and he also worked from home, but Ally enjoyed making big breakfasts and today was no different. She started up the coffee and pulled the ingredients from the fridge and cupboards to make omelets and hash browns. She then made some freshly-squeezed orange juice and set the table. In moments like these, she thought of children running into the room, running around the island, sliding on the wood floors in their socks, with Ally telling them to be careful and wash up for breakfast, possibly breaking up a fight between the siblings. She wanted at least two children, after growing up an only child. As close as she was with her mom, she longed to have a brother or sister. Her children would have cousins, something Ally also didn't have, as a result of her mom being an only child and her father being absent from her life.

Oliver walked sleepily into the kitchen, rubbing his eyes with the back of his hands.

"Good morning, beautiful. You're up with the sunshine."

"Can't sleep. I'm so excited!"

"Smells great in here, love."

"Hope it tastes as good as it smells. Are you off today?"

"Yes. We're heading up today to check into the hotel."

"Good. The girls are doing that as well and then going to the cottage to oversee the set up."

"Are you staying with me tonight?"

"No, I'm staying with Sadie," Ally said stepping up on her tiptoes to give him a kiss. "I told you that."

"I know, just checking," he said with a grin. "I'm used to you being here all the time. I'm going to miss you," Oliver whined, squeezing her hip.

"We'll survive!" Ally laughed.

"Yes, but doesn't mean I have to like it," he pouted.

Ally dished out their meal at the breakfast table in front of the large bay window facing onto the back patio. She gave Oliver a kiss on the cheek and sat down across from him.

"So far so good, eh?" Ally asked.

"Breakfast is amazing."

"No, I meant us, living together."

"Ally, it's more than amazing."

"Good." She said with a grin, stuffing a piece of toast in her mouth. She made him smile.

After breakfast was done and cleaned up, Ally and Oliver enjoyed some time together before packing and going their separate ways. Oliver was driving up to the Muskokas and checking into a hotel, while Ally was going to Sadie's to help her pack before driving her up to the cottage.

Ally arrived at Sadie's, knocked, and then let herself in with her own set of keys. She called around the empty condo and eventually found Sadie in the tub.

"How's our bride-to-be?" Ally called through the door.

"Come in," Sadie responded.

"Okay," Ally said hesitantly, laughed and slowly opened the door. Unsure of what she would see, she asked with eyes closed, "Are you decent?"

"Yes, silly." Sadie responded, up to her eyeballs in bubbles.

"You're too funny. Did you use the whole bottle of bubble bath?" Ally went and sat on the edge of the large Jacuzzi tub.

"It's not a bath unless I do."

"So, how ya' doing?"

"I'm fantastic," Sadie answered, without hesitation. "Levi left about an hour ago. You know, Ally, I feel the same way I did a year ago when we finally told each other how we felt. I simply adore him."

"I know you do."

"It seems too good to be true."

"It's not, it's really happening."

"I just feel so lucky."

"You are, but so is he. You both went through a lot of duds before you realized the perfect person was standing right in front of you."

"Yes. I'm so happy you and Oliver found your way to each other, even if there were some detours along the way."

"Me too." Ally cupped bubbles in her palm and blew them across the tub at Sadie. "What can I do? Anything you need to me to do while you're finishing up?"

"Nope. We filled Levi's car earlier and he's headed up to the cottage to drop it all off today. The wedding planner will be there at the crack of dawn with a crew setting up."

"Okay, well, no rush, I have some calls to make and will see you when you get out."

"Won't be long."

"What about your wedding dress?"

"My parents have it. They're coming up tonight to stay at the cottage as well. Do you have your dress?"

"You bet. I also have Piper's and Sam's. Not taking any chances!" Ally and Sadie laughed as Ally closed the bathroom door behind her. They knew what Piper could be like. She was often flighty and forgetful, in an endearing way. Ally went to make some calls to her mom, to the store, and couldn't help but make a call to Oliver to see how his drive was going.

Before long the girls were headed up north. Tunes were blaring, they were nibbling on licorice and both were sipping on their favourite drinks from the local cafe. First stop was to pick up Piper and then Samantha. Their dates were going to join them in the evening at the rehearsal party. Piper was bringing her on and off again boyfriend, Diego, and Samantha was bringing her friend and agent, Josh. Catriona and Jones were also making their way up north and spending the weekend up there for the wedding.

The wedding rehearsal took place at a restaurant that overlooked the lake; they would be saying their vows tomorrow afternoon in front of that same breathtaking lake that meant so much to them. Tonight they enjoyed a delicious meal and a few drinks before calling it an early night in preparation for the big day. Close family and friends were in attendance. There was nothing but love in the air.

Ally watched as Sadie and Levi had a touching moment saying good night. He was tucking her hair behind her ear, his finger lingering on her cheek, speaking softly, kissing her on the tip of her nose. Sadie put her arms around his neck pulling him in closer, a smile from ear to ear. It made her think of the book launch party where Sadie professed the truth about her feelings for Levi and he reciprocated with planting a kiss on her. The crowd cheered that it was about time.

That's also the night when Ally realized she really liked Oliver, a lot, and it had made her nervous. She had fled that night and hid away for a couple of weeks. She would never do that again. She allowed herself to love and be loved.

Oliver came up behind Ally, kissing her on her neck, interrupting her thoughts.

"What's on your mind, love?"

"Just thinking about Sadie, Levi…" Ally said, turning her body towards him and looking up into his brilliant blue eyes. "Thinking about you and me."

Oliver leaned down and planted a soft, slow kiss on Ally. The kind that usually followed with Ally taking his hand and leading him off somewhere quiet. The kind that still made her knees go soft, a flutter in her lower belly, and a warmth in her cheeks.

"Mmmmm…." Ally hummed. "I can't wait until tomorrow night."

"Me too." Oliver winked and wrapped her in a big hug. "Have a good night's sleep, love. I'll call you in the morning."

They said their goodbyes. Ally caught up with the bride and bridesmaids while Oliver corralled the groom and groomsmen. Time to get everyone back to the hotel and get a good sleep for the big day. He wasn't one to blow a party, but this group knew how to have a good time and he didn't want to risk anyone being in rough shape. Not on his watch.

Chapter 29

Wedding

Ally and the bridesmaids, Samantha and Piper walked down the aisle amongst the trees on an unseasonably warm, fall day. The weather couldn't have been better if they had ordered it. The trees were filled with fall colours. The lake was in view, crisp and clear, with the odd bird flying overhead. The chairs weren't set up traditionally, but in groupings, with a winding aisle through the trees. The girls looked stunning in their grey-blue dresses and burnt orange coloured roses. They came to stand across the aisle from the men, already standing tall, looking like they stepped out of GQ.

Ally could feel Oliver looking at her the entire walk down the aisle. She gave him an extra sashay before coming to a stop at the front. Then she gave him a cheeky smile and wink when they made eye contact. He made her giggle as he pretended to fall to his knees.

Sweet Thing by Van Morrison hung in the air, a perfect song for Sadie to make her walk towards Levi on the arm of her dad. Urns of Sadie's favourite flowers were placed throughout, and soy candles made with essential oils of cedarwood and orange burned. Twinkling lights hung from the lower branches making it magical. Everyone came to their feet for the bride's entrance.

The guests gasped as Sadie came into view. She was breathtaking. The delicate ivory lace of her wedding dress was hugging her body in all of the right places; her healthy, fit physique from years of yoga and running, a perfect match for the style of the dress. Her makeup was dewy and natural to enhance her flawless features. Like a bohemian princess, her long, wavy blonde hair was pulled to one side and one big, sunshine-coloured country rose was tucked behind her ear. She had her arms looped through her dad's. Her bouquet was made of more country roses in shades of fall, including yellows, reds, and oranges.

Levi was standing tall and proud. He was breathtaking in his own right, with his hair lightly slicked back, clean-shaven and in a tailored, navy suit, with a white shirt and navy tie, with a country rose pinned on his lapel to match Sadie's. The two could give any Hollywood power couple a run for their money. If you looked closely enough, you could see Levi's jaw clench ever so slightly, likely a tool to stop him from crying. His hands tightly clasped in front of him. He didn't take his eyes off of her, not even for a second. He gave her a broad smile and one single tear escaped his eye.

Sadie looked at each guest along her walk; she had a way of making every single person feel as though they were special. Her eyes came to rest on her future husband, her eyes misting over, her mouth widening into a smile to match his.

Once the ceremony started, Ally peeked around Sadie and up into the eyes of Oliver, who was looking at her from across the aisle. He gave her a wink, mouthed that she looked beautiful, and then added I love you. She melted. His dark hair was also slightly slicked back for the occasion, and his face clean shaven. The colour of the navy suit along with his thick lashes emphasized his crystal-blue eyes and handsome looks. He gave her a smile that made her knees weak, and she instantly thought about the kiss they shared last night. She couldn't wait to be in his arms again.

The personal ceremony finished with cheers from the guests and was followed by short sweet speeches and dinner with a party in the large cottage. Furniture had been moved that morning to make space for the tables for the close knit guests that were in attendance. Only their very best friends and family were there.

Once dinner was wrapped up, the wedding planning crew moved the tables to make way for a dance floor. The couple's first dance was to the song "Into the Mystic". The happy couple whispered into each other's ears, sharing laughs and tears in those three minutes, with Levi holding Sadie tight around her waist and Sadie's arms draped around his neck. Friends and family took photos, standing by to witness the day they had always hoped would come.

When the wedding song finished, 'Better Man' by Paolo Nutini began to play and others were urged to take to the dance floor with them.

"Excuse me miss, may I have this dance?" Oliver asked, leaning down to speak into Ally's ear. His breath on her earlobe still caused a reaction to this day, sending tingles down her spine and landing in her lower belly.

"I would love to," Ally answered, turning and placing her hand in his. He pulled her in close and they enjoyed a quiet dance, letting their bodies speak for them. It was one of the only times they didn't talk or were trying to make each other laugh. It was out of character and yet felt so comfortable. Ally and Oliver had reached the point in their relationship where they both knew where they were headed. Their unspoken words defined the love that the two shared and the happiness they had found together. They knew it was only a matter time before they would also be exchanging vows.

The wine flowed and the guests enjoyed themselves; no one needed to worry about driving at the end of the night. The music was amazing, a personal mix made by Sadie and Levi. Friends and family were telling stories, hugging, dancing; laughter filled the quiet spaces in the air. The large cottage was surrounded on the outside by the twinkling lights still hanging in the trees, which provided a pretty view from the large windows.

Sometime in the early morning hours, after more than a good time, the guests made their way by limos to the hotel, leaving the newly married couple to celebrate in one of the places that meant so much to them. They had been going to the cottage together for years, long before they became a couple. Levi had bought the cottage with the intention of sharing it one day with Sadie.

Oliver held Ally's hand all the way to the hotel. They sat in silence, smiling at each other when they caught the other looking.

"One day, my love," Oliver said, kissing the top of Ally's hand.

"Yes. I would love that." Ally answered. Oliver pulled her into his side, kissing the top of her head.

"That wasn't the proposal. But it will come, my love. I promise you now that when I make it, you'll know. I'll take you somewhere special, or completely surprise you with a grand gesture," Oliver said candidly and genuinely.

"Ollie, for the record, I wouldn't care how you did it."

"I know, but I'll at least have the ring with me." He turned his body towards her to make his point. Grasping her hands in his, he said, "I'm caught up in this amazing night, and I'm saying more than I should. It will happen, my love. And when it does, it will be a surprise." Ally knew what he meant. It wasn't that he was back tracking on a proposal and never going to ask. He simply couldn't help himself in the moment by saying what he was thinking; that it was going to happen, one day.

"I know, Ollie," she said, leaning up to give him a kiss. "It was an absolutely amazing night. I'm feeling very romantic myself. It definitely got me thinking about a BIG DAY in the future. It highlighted how much you mean to me."

"Well, they sure planned that day perfectly, didn't they?"

"Yes. They planned it around where they love to be, what they love, and who they love."

"Makes for a pretty good recipe," he said.

The limo came to a stop out front of the hotel. Oliver got out before the driver had a chance, holding his hand out for Ally, helping her out of the car. Tipping the driver, he leaned down and scooped up the petite redhead who was now giggling, and carried her into the building.

Chapter 30

Movies

"This is brilliant!" Ally exclaimed to Sadie and Samantha.

"I couldn't wish for anyone else to play the heroine than you, Samantha," Sadie said.

"I'm thrilled!! I know you had a hand in this Sadie, and I'm so thankful," Samantha gushed. "People in my circle are talking about this movie and want to be in it. They're calling this the romantic comedy of 2019."

Samantha was speaking of none other than Sadie's first book that was being turned into a movie. Sadie was ecstatic when she had been approached by the movie company. Being her first novel, it was a special story that led to her success as a New York Times Best Selling Author.

Eventually, it also led her to meet her agent, and now husband, Levi. Levi was working through the details of the film and book rights day and night as everyone was excited to get this project going.

Samantha had been chosen for the female lead, and the male lead was still under review. The production company had compiled a list of actors and actresses. They worked out a deal that Sadie had the final choice.

"No need to thank me. The producers had a short list and your name was at the top. I simply yelled YES YES YES when I saw it." The girls laughed and leaned forward to clink their glasses together. Samantha wasn't tied to any creative collaborations at the moment and the press events had slowed down from the last film she was in. It was perfect timing for this movie to come along. Samantha meant what she had said; she had hoped she would have a shot at this movie. From what Sadie knew, filming could begin within the next couple of months. They had to secure the male lead who was hopefully going to be another heavy hitter from Hollywood. Samantha wasn't lying when she said it would be the biggest romantic comedy of 2019.

They were having a girls night at Sadie and Levi's new home that they had bought after the wedding more than six months ago. Levi and Oliver were playing poker with business guests from Oliver's firm. Both Ally and Samantha were going to spend the night.

There was a ton of room in this beautiful, large Arts and Crafts style home that had been through renovations before they bought it. There was very little for them to do except move in. They had more than enough furniture from both of their previous homes. Having been best friends for years, they had picked out all of their furniture together. Sadie was sad leaving the penthouse apartment that she had designed, but they both wanted a place to start fresh for the two of them.

They had found the perfect spot just outside of the city on a large piece of property with a small barn. Sadie couldn't wait to start her vegetable garden and get a few dogs. Levi had plans for a pool and was working with landscapers. Both of them had plans for children. They were hoping they could share news soon.

The girls were sitting around the oversized kitchen island, music playing from the Bose on the kitchen counter. Sadie had brought her signature style, turquoise and grey colour palette, evident throughout the home.

"Who's going to play Alistair?" Ally asked Samantha, referring to the male lead from the book.

"I haven't heard yet. There are a couple of guys up for the role." Sadie said.

"Who?" Ally asked.

"I immediately nixed Nate," Sadie reassured Ally.

"Thanks," Ally said sheepishly, knowing it would just be too much of a strain on her relationship with Oliver to have to deal with Nate again.

"They told me that William James was interested, as well as Nick Stone," Sadie said, immediately looking for Samantha's reaction.

Samantha got up to get another glass of wine. "I heard Nick Stone was up for consideration. I hate to say this, and I know that it's very unprofessional of me, but I don't like that guy."

"What?! Nick Stone!!! He would be amazing! So hot!" Ally squealed.

"Oh he is pretty, I know. I'll give you that," Samantha answered, settling herself back down on the couch.

"How did you get so lucky? You know, besides working hard and all that." Ally teased.

"Hmph." Samantha mused. "He has an ego. He thinks he's God's gift. You saw him at the restaurant."

"Oh, I saw him!" Ally squealed. "But, don't they all have egos?"

"At least actors? They need to have confidence, no?" Sadie added, grabbing chips and the fresh guacamole she had made.

"Believe it or not there are some who are down to earth."

"So he didn't leave that good of an impression on you. Like I said before, we don't know the circumstances surrounding that woman he was with," Sadie offered.

"Maybe he thought that was the way to impress you," Ally suggested. But Samantha just shook her head in defiance.

"There is confidence and then there is narcissism. And there is having a girlfriend or not having one. It is that simple," Samantha stated.

Ally looked at Sadie, knowing exactly what she was thinking. He would be perfect for the role!

Sadie sat back watching Samantha. She thought about the story and what would make the most sense for the characters. The way the story unfolds, it would benefit from this tension that she could see in Samantha right now. She knew in time Sam would warm up to Nick, and if she didn't, she was an actor, and had enough professionalism that she would figure it out.

Nonchalantly Sadie picked up her phone and texted Levi. *Tell them I want Nick Stone for the role.*

Levi responded right away, *Will do. How are things there, babe? Miss you and our home.* He was such a sap and Sadie loved it.

We're having fun, and a good gab about the movie. Seems like Sam would not agree with me about Nick. In fact, I think she will be livid.

And you want him anyway? Didn't you just say Sam didn't agree?

Yes, but he's perfect.

But she doesn't like him?

She can't stand him!

And you want him?

He's perfect!

Should I be jealous? Levi responded, teasing.

Perfect for the role and perfect for Sam.

Perfect.

I know they'll be perfect together.

Perfect, Levi repeated.

Sparks will fly Levi! Just you watch. They may be for the wrong reasons at first, but I know they'll have amazing chemistry together.

You sound confident, and when you sound confident it is the right answer.

I'm so confident! Sadie answered.

Okay, I'll make some calls, Levi texted back.

Thank you. I love you.

Love you too. Now I need to go kick Oliver's ass in this hand.

Sadie winked at Ally. Ally picked up her phone and saw a message from Oliver.

Nick Stone and Samantha, eh? Should be good. Levi had already told Oliver. Ally shook her head and laughed.

It will be amazing! Ally texted back.

"So, wedding bells must be around the corner, Ally?" Samantha said to her with a grin, changing the subject.

"We've talked about it."

"You're holding out on us," Sadie gasped exaggeratingly

"We talked after your wedding. We know it's going to happen. You know Oliver; it will be some over-the-top grand gesture, like Levi," Ally pointed out.

"He did take you to Paris for your second date," Sadie teased.

"See! I told him that was extravagant!" Ally laughed at the embellishment, although Sadie wasn't that far off.

Just then there was a knock on the door. The three girls looked at each other. It was odd to have someone knock on their door in the country. Sadie went to look out the window and see who it could be. Samantha and Ally heard the front door open and got up to see what was going on.

"Ally, can you come here?" Confused, Ally set down her wine and followed Samantha to the door. A man with a headset on, in a tux stood in the doorway. A noisy hum came from outside.

"Miss Ally, can you come with me?" Ally looked beyond him to see a helicopter. *What the heck? A freaking helicopter!*

Sitting inside of it was Oliver, also in a tux, holding a huge bouquet of flowers. He waved.

"Oh my!" Samantha squealed, "Here's your grand gesture!"

"Have a wonderful night, Ally. You deserve all of this and more!" Sadie said with a knowing smile, having been part of the guise from the get-go.

The girls gave Ally a big hug and sent her out the door. She was wearing Oliver's oversized hoodie and her sweatpants for a night in with the girls. Now she was off in a helicopter with Oliver who was wearing a tux! Her tummy was full of butterflies thinking about the evening that lay ahead, but she wasn't going to let that detail bother her. As she entered the helicopter, Oliver greeted her with a kiss. He lay a huge box across her lap, telling her she could change at their next stop. Inside the box was a little black dress and high heels.

"Oliver!"

"Enjoy the view, my love. Toronto looks beautiful at night."

"Oliver, this is amazing." Ally said, hugging his arm. She could barely contain herself. Oliver planted a kiss on her forehead.

The helicopter took them for a scenic view of the Toronto skyline, then came to land at the

Toronto Island airport where a private jet was waiting.

"There's our plane. You can get dressed on it."

Ally's jaw dropped. It continued to hit the floor when she entered the jet to see more flowers and hear "April in Paris" by Louis Armstrong and Ella Fitzgerald playing.

"Are we…" Ally couldn't finish her sentence.

"Of course we are," Oliver answered. "There should be everything you need in the bathroom to get ready. You can go once the seatbelt sign is off."

Ally sat down beside him, buckled up, and turned, her mouth still ajar.

"I love you, Ally. I'm going to try to make this night a night you'll never forget."

"We could get off this plane right now and you would have accomplished that."

"Yes, but what would be the fun in that? I have many more surprises up my sleeve."

"More than a helicopter, a jet, and Paris?!"

"Oh love, that's only the beginning." He said with his charming smile.

Holding her hand tightly, he kissed the top of it as the jet made its way down the runway and lifted off to begin the fairy tale that awaited them both.

The End.

Please sign up for my newsletter to stay up to date on new releases and book signings.

For more information please visit jillbreugem.com

Also available from Jill Breugem:

Read Between the Lines

92997423R00167

Made in the USA
Columbia, SC
03 April 2018